THE SAPPHIRE

Cass, a talented jeweller, wants a quiet life after having helped to solve a murder case. But life is anything but dull while she lives with her mother, an eccentric witch with a penchant for attracting trouble. Now Cass's father, who left the family when she was five, is back on the scene — as well as handsome detective Noel Raven, with whom Cass has an electrifying relationship. As dangers both worldly and paranormal threaten Cass and those she loves, will they be strong enough to stand together and prevail?

FAY CUNNINGHAM

◆

THE SAPPHIRE
The Moonstones Trilogy

Complete and Unabridged

LINFORD
Leicester

First published in Great Britain in 2015

First Linford Edition
published 2016

A catalogue record for this book is available
from the British Library.

ISBN 978–1–4448–2873–3

Published by
F. A. Thorpe (Publishing)
Anstey, Leicestershire

Set by Words & Graphics Ltd.
Anstey, Leicestershire
Printed and bound in Great Britain by
T. J. International Ltd., Padstow, Cornwall

This book is printed on acid-free paper

1

Cass looked up in annoyance at the knock on her door. She had been in the middle of wrapping a beautiful blue jasper cabochon in gold wire and the knock upset her concentration. The only person likely to knock on her door at this time of day was Noel Raven, and she really didn't want to talk to him right this minute.

Sighing, she got to her feet and walked across her studio to open the door, but the person standing outside and looking at her rather apprehensively wasn't the detective. The woman standing in the shadow of the rowan tree was probably in her late forties, dark-haired, petite, and quite attractive. Her soft brown eyes regarded Cass worriedly.

'I'm sorry, I've obviously caught you in the middle of something important.

1

Liz gave me your address, but I should have called first.'

'Liz sent you?' Cass felt embarrassed that her irritation had shown so plainly on her face. She held the door wide. 'Please come in. I'm not doing anything that can't wait a little while.'

The woman walked into Cass's studio and looked around the converted garage with interest. The area was quite big, with shelves filling two walls and a workbench under the window. A swivel chair stood in front of a cluttered desk and a small sofa filled most of the remaining space. Her eyes took in the workbench and the tools Cass had been using.

'This is where you work and I've interrupted you. I'm so sorry. I should have phoned and made an appointment, but Liz said it would be OK just to call round.'

'It's fine, really. Please sit down.' Cass waved the woman to a seat before she could apologise again. She didn't like people calling on her while she was

2

working. The studio was her sanctuary, but she was always prepared to make a few exceptions. 'You're a friend of Liz Portman?'

'I'm a nurse. We work together at the hospital.' She sat rather awkwardly on Cass's little sofa. 'Oh, my name's Rachel, by the way. Rachel Saunders.'

Cass found the woman's nervousness puzzling. 'Is this something to do with my work? Do you want a piece of jewellery made?'

'Not exactly. I feel really silly now. You work with precious stones and gold and things, and this is well, it's just a repair really, not something you'll want to take on.'

'I was just going to make a cup of tea.' Cass was intrigued now, and quite glad of the interruption. 'I'll make us tea and you can explain what it is you want me to do. If I don't want to do it, I'll tell you. How does that sound?'

Rachel smiled. 'Thank you. I know I go on a bit when I'm flustered. Tea would be lovely.' She looked at the jewellery Cass had on display in her glass cabinet. 'All this stuff looks really expensive.'

'Some of it is.' Cass filled the electric kettle at her small sink and turned it on. Luckily she had two clean mugs. 'But some of it is quite reasonable considering every piece is unique. I work mainly with semi-precious stones in their natural state, uncut. It's the cutting that costs the money.' She dropped a teabag in each mug and waited for her ancient kettle to boil. It made such a noise it was impossible to talk until she had filled the mugs and handed one to Rachel.

'I was given a necklace,' Rachel said. 'It's really cheap, I think, but it has some pretty stones in it that I quite like.' She took a breath. 'I'll start from the beginning. I was on holiday in America a couple of weeks ago. My aunt died and left me some money, a few thousand pounds, so I went to Miami. I've always wanted to go there. You know — you see Miami Beach on

TV and it looks great, and then you want to go there. Anyway, I met a guy who gave me this necklace just before I left for home. He was really sweet and he meant well, and he looked OK in a T-shirt and shorts . . . ' She stopped for breath again. 'Anyway, he was coming back to England at the same time as me so we were going to travel home together. I was looking forward to the company because it's a long flight and, like I said, he seemed nice.' She took a sip of her tea and smiled ruefully. 'But he got sick at the airport and disappeared into the men's room. Our flight was called and he hadn't come back out so I travelled back alone. I don't suppose he ever intended to come back with me, although he did look quite sick, so I don't really know. The story of my life, men walking out on me.'

Cass waited a few minutes. 'What about the necklace? Do you have it with you?'

Rachel laughed, obviously embarrassed. 'I'm sorry, you're busy working and I'm telling you my life story.'

'Do you want me to have a look at the necklace?' Cass prompted.

The woman gave a little sigh. 'Yes, please. It's broken and Liz thought you might be able to repair it.' She picked up her handbag and took out a large envelope, handing it to Cass.

Cass undid the flap and peered inside. Then she tipped the necklace out onto her workbench. The setting was made of some cheap silver-coloured metal. A chain with five small flowers graduated in size, each one joined by a metal link. In the middle of each flower a deep blue stone sat slightly off-centre. The middle stone was round and about the size of a five pence piece; the other four were smaller but perfectly matched. Cass saw at once that one of the links had broken, taking one of the flower petals with it and leaving the necklace in two halves.

'I know it's only a cheap necklace,' Rachel said. 'But I really like the stones.'

'I don't think I can solder it back together,' Cass said. 'If I do, it will break again, and you'll be back here to have it fixed again. You're right about the stones, though. They are pretty.' She bent down for a closer look and felt a little jolt of surprise. 'Really clear,' she said softly, 'and a lovely colour. It might be worth having them reset.'

'Oh, do you think so? I'm so glad!' Rachel couldn't keep the relief out of her voice. 'He was such a nice guy. Well, I thought so at the time, but even if he really was sick I doubt he'll get in touch with me again.'

'He might,' Cass said. She had a feeling the 'nice guy' might want to be reunited with his necklace at some point. 'He must have thought a lot of you to buy you the necklace.'

Rachel laughed. 'You can get an idea how much he thought of me by his choice of jewellery. He was really pleased with it though. He gave it to me at the airport, put it on for me and everything. I really thought . . . ' Her voice tailed off. 'How much would it cost to have the stones reset?'

'I can set them in flowers made of silver or gold wire. The necklace won't look the same but it will last a lot longer. The stones are a fair size, so how about I design a three-stone pendant and use the two remaining stones for earrings? If you give me an idea of how much you want to spend, I can keep within your budget.' She picked up the necklace and held it up to the light. 'I think the stones will look amazing when I unstick them from this cheap alloy. They deserve better.'

Rachel got to her feet. 'Thank you. I rather fancy gold for the setting. I've got a bit left from my aunt's money, so I can afford it. This is going to be fun.' She smiled at Cass. 'Forget the cost and make those pretty stones look as good as you can. I've never had any really nice jewellery before.'

'I'll do several designs with different prices,' Cass said, 'and you can choose which one you want. I'll be happy to do the drawings free of charge. Like you said, it will be fun turning the ugly duckling into a swan.' She held up her hand as Rachel headed for the door. 'Wait a minute. I'll give you a receipt for the necklace.'

'Oh, don't worry about that. It's not as if it's worth much.' Rachel laughed. 'Besides, I know where you live.'

Cass closed the door behind Rachel and picked up the necklace. She was desperate to have a look at the stones through her loupe. She had to be mistaken. No one in their right mind would stick five perfect, dark blue sapphires onto a cheap piece of metal. But fifteen minutes later she came to the conclusion that someone had done exactly that. As far as she could tell the sapphires were superb, and particularly well-cut. It had taken her a while to unstick the stones from the setting. She had no idea what glue had been used or how it might react when it came in contact with another chemical. Sapphires are notoriously tough, second in hardness to a diamond, but she knew there are some chemicals that can harm them.

If the woman had inadvertently smuggled the stones out of America, Cass wondered where the sapphires had come from in the first place. They certainly weren't indigenous to Miami, although she knew sapphires had been mined in other parts of the US. Some of the best stones in the deepest blue, like the one she held in her hand, originally came from Burma or Kashmir.

The sapphire felt cool, almost cold. She knew the stone supposedly had magical powers, but she had never seen any proof of this. Always slightly cynical about the power of gemstones, her doubts had been put to the test recently when a ruby helped save her life.

With a sigh, she dropped the blue stones into a velvet bag. Now what? She had no proof the stones had been obtained dishonestly. Perhaps setting them in a cheap necklace was someone's idea of a joke, or perhaps Rachel's

Miami acquaintance had no idea the stones were real sapphires. She didn't know how much he had paid for the necklace. He might be a millionaire in disguise and could have paid a fortune for the gems. All she was doing at the moment was speculating.

Her thoughts turned to Noel Raven, the new detective inspector at Norton police station. He had telephoned her several times since their encounter with the sociopath who had murdered her mother's lover. But after her lack of response his calls had tapered off, and for the last few weeks she had heard nothing from him. Not that she cared. Not one bit. Noel Raven was trouble, a distraction she could do without. Her jewellery business was booming and she kept telling herself she didn't have time for distractions.

She put the empty mugs in the little sink, pushed the bag of sapphires into the pocket of her jeans, and opened the door leading into the main house. She needed another viewpoint. Without

11

even thinking about it, she made her way straight to the kitchen where she knew she would find her mother.

The room was part of the old house and hadn't changed much over the years. The units were new, and so was the American style fridge/freezer, but the floor still glowed with the old terracotta tiles, and the refectory table and high-back chairs had come with the house.

Pandora Moon was sitting at the table, her feet propped up on the cross-bar. She was a tiny woman, wearing her usual colourful kaftan, her silver hair falling almost to her shoulders, her feet bare. A frown creased her forehead as she stared at the screen of her laptop. She had a look of intense concentration on her face, but she looked up when she heard Cass come into the room.

'I'm having a problem with the mandrake I bought online. I'm trying to find another source.'

'Mandrake?' Cass walked across the large kitchen to stand behind her mother. 'Isn't that supposed to shriek when you pull it up?'

Dora shook her head. 'I don't intend to harvest my own. That's why I order it online. Can you put the kettle on, Cassie? I haven't had time to make a cup of tea.'

'Why mandrake?' Cass asked as she filled the kettle. 'It's poisonous. You can't use it in your potions.'

'It's not poisonous in small doses; it's a hallucinogen and a tranquilizer, perfect for a good night's sleep, and it's also a good general painkiller. Besides, I know how to make it safe.'

'I'm sure you do, Mother.' Cass put two teabags in a small teapot and poured on water. 'Just be careful, that's all. I wouldn't want you to kill anyone.'

Dora hadn't left the house for the last six months. She had been attacked in the street by a gang of youths and the trauma had left her with anxiety problems. At least, that was what Cass called it. Dora was convinced she was under a spell cast by her warlock

13

husband, a spell to keep her safely inside the house. Now she ran an online business from home, selling recipes for herbal medicines. Her ingredients were personally customized to suit each individual, and Cass knew her mother made quite a lot of money. The fact that Dora advertised herself as a witch probably helped. Cass didn't believe in magic, or witches and warlocks, but recent events had shaken her disbelief a little. Maybe there really were more things in heaven and earth than she had dreamed of.

She handed Dora a mug of tea and sat down at the table. 'You've got a problem with your mandrake and I've got a problem with some stones, but mine is more of a moral dilemma than a physical problem.' She took the bag out of her pocket and tipped the sapphires onto the table. 'What do you think?'

'Of the stones?' Dora reached out and picked up the largest. 'Beautiful. They look perfect to me. What's the problem?'

'I think they look perfect, too. That's the problem. The woman who gave them to me thinks they are bits of blue glass and worthless. Some guy in Miami gave her a cheap necklace with these stones stuck onto it. She wants me to design a new setting for them.'

'I still don't understand why there's a problem. If the stones are sapphires rather than blue glass, they deserve a pretty setting. Do you think there's something illegal going on?'

'I'm wondering what five perfect sapphires are doing in a cheap setting. I'm also wondering why someone gave them to Rachel Saunders to bring back to England.'

Dora looked puzzled for a moment. 'Are you talking about smuggling? Someone bringing precious stones into the country without paying tax? It seems an unusual way to go about smuggling gemstones, but I suppose it could work. Is the woman involved?'

Cass shook her head. 'No. At least, I'm pretty sure she's not part of anything illegal. She works with Liz at the hospital. No way is she going to be involved in a scheme to smuggle sapphires through customs.'

'Did the man who gave her the necklace arrange to meet her again? He's going want his sapphires back.'

'He was supposed to travel back with her, but he got sick at the airport and had to stay behind. I don't know whether that was all part of the game or if it was genuine. He told the woman — whose name is Rachel, by the way — that he'd contact her here in England, but she doesn't think he really meant it. She thinks it was just a holiday romance and she won't see him again.'

'If the man's a smuggler, she'll definitely see him again,' Dora said. 'I would imagine he meant to travel back with his necklace so he could keep an eye on it. As it is, his girlfriend has already given the stones to you. She could have put them in the nearest rubbish bin for all he knows.'

'So why didn't he ask for them back

when he got sick? Rachel would have been only too pleased to hand over the necklace. She didn't particularly like it.' Cass thought for a minute. 'But he had no other way of getting the sapphires out of the country, did he? He couldn't put them in his case and risk getting searched, and he couldn't wear the necklace himself, so he had to trust her.'

'He was taking a big chance. It would have been simpler to pay the duty. He'd still have made a profit.'

'Not if the sapphires were stolen,' Cass said quietly. 'The airport staff would have a list of stolen items. They'd be looking out for them, hidden in a bag or suitcase. But they wouldn't be expecting to see them round Rachel's neck. They were hidden in plain sight. It's quite clever, really.'

Dora picked up the stones and dropped them back into the bag one by one. 'Get in touch with Noel, Cassie. Let him handle it. If you're right, it could get dangerous. You're the one with the man's sapphires, so it's you he'll be coming after.'

'I can't bring anyone else into this, can I? Not without asking Rachel first. Technically, the necklace is hers.'

'Are you one hundred percent sure the stones are sapphires? Fakes can fool experts these days.'

Cass shook her head. 'No, I'm not one hundred percent sure. I can't be without a few more tests. But they feel right. I think I'd know if they were fakes.'

'I think you would, too,' Dora said, 'and telling Rachel could put her in danger. While she thinks she has a cheap necklace set with pieces of blue glass, she's no threat to the smugglers. Give the stones to Noel, Cassie. If you keep them here you may be putting us both in danger.'

Cass sighed. Her mother was clever; she knew Cass might be prepared to risk her own life, but no way would she risk her mother's as well. 'All right, I'll phone him, but just to ask his advice.'

'Yes, you do that.' Dora smiled. 'Noel Raven will enjoy giving you advice.'

Cass scowled. 'I should stop while you're ahead, Mother, otherwise I might change my mind.'

She picked up the phone before she really did change her mind. Noel Raven scared her, and it took a lot to scare her. He had brought her back from the dead a few months ago, but she had no idea how he had managed to do that. She didn't think he knew exactly what had happened, either, which was the scary part. Whenever he got close to her, there was an electric charge in the air that made her feel strangely fragile and defenceless — not a feeling she liked particularly, so she stayed out of his way. She wasn't used to feeling vulnerable. She had no recollection of ever having a father, and her mother wasn't exactly normal, so she had grown up well able to take care of herself. She had run her own business since giving up her job in the admin department of the local hospital and was beginning to gain a reputation for designing beautiful hand-made jewellery. She didn't need Noel Raven.

He answered on the third ring. 'Cassandra. How nice to hear from you. I thought I must have done something to upset you. Apart from saving your life, of course.' She didn't answer immediately and she heard him laugh. 'What can I do for you?'

'I have a problem with a client who brought me some jewellery to reset. There might be something illegal going on. Can I talk to you off the record?'

'Ooh, I'm not sure about that. We can't talk off the record on the phone, can we? Anyone could be listening in. So it might involve a visit to your house. Do you think you can cope with that? Otherwise you'll have to meet me for a drink later on this evening. I'll be at the Rising Sun.'

Why did he always make her feel as if she were being manipulated? 'Fine. I'll meet you at the pub. What time?'

'Eight o'clock in the main bar.'

He hung up before she had time to change her mind. At least he hadn't suggested he pick her up from home. Whenever he met up with Dora, they got on to the subject of witchcraft. Noel seemed fascinated by spells and potions, and her mother didn't need encouraging; she was weird enough already.

Cass put down the phone to find Dora watching her with a smile. 'What?'

'He's managed to talk you into a date. I thought you weren't going to see him again.'

'It's not a date. I don't want him in my studio, and if he comes here you'll both start talking rubbish. He can buy me a drink, I'll explain about the stones, and then I'll come home.'

'What else would you do?' Dora asked innocently.

Cass scowled. 'This is just about the gemstones, Mother. Nothing more. It's not a social occasion. I certainly don't want to walk all the way into town to meet him. It was your idea.'

Dora raised her hands. 'I'm agreeing

with you, Cassie. If talking to the man on the phone gets you this worked up, meeting him is bound to be a disaster. I'm sorry I suggested it.'

Cass looked at her mother suspiciously. She was never quite sure if Dora was trying to wind her up. 'No, I'll go. It'll be fine.'

Dora smiled. 'Of course it will.' She closed the lid of her laptop. 'I think I might try growing my own mandrake, but I'm not sure how dangerous that would be. There are stories about people dying when they hear the mandrake scream.'

'Earplugs,' Cass said. 'And a knitted balaclava with earmuffs on top. You might look a bit peculiar, but at least you'll be safe.'

'Go and get ready for your date,' Dora said. 'You've got glue or something all down your front.'

2

Sitting at his desk at the police station, Noel Raven smiled to himself. He put the phone back in its rest and stretched his long legs out under his desk. He had been pretty sure Cass wouldn't be able to keep him at arm's length forever, and he had been right.

'What put that smug look on your face?' Brenda asked as she walked into his office carrying a mug of tea. 'You look like the proverbial cat.'

Noel smiled. 'I'm taking Cassandra Moon out for a drink tonight.'

'Did you phone her or did she phone you?'

His smile got broader. 'She phoned me.'

'To ask you out for a drink?'

'Don't sound so surprised. Women have been known to ask me out for a drink before.'

23

'Not Cassandra Moon. You scare her.'

He looked genuinely puzzled. 'How can I scare her? I saved her life.'

'That's why you scare her. You brought her back from the dead, and you don't know how you did it.' Brenda picked up the stack of files lying on his desk and headed for the door. 'That's enough to scare anyone.'

Noel frowned as he watched his senior police detective leave the room. Was that true? Was Cass really frightened of him? The thought had never entered his head, but maybe it should have done. Cassandra Moon didn't believe in miracles or magic, and what had happened between them had to be one or the other.

He got to the Rising Sun early so he could be sure of getting a table and found one on the far side of the room away from the bar. With a bit of luck they might not have to shout to one another. The pub was one of those androgynous places, neither old nor new, neither smart nor shabby, just the way he liked his pubs.

He spotted her the moment she walked in the door and felt the familiar tug in his gut. She was like a magnet. They had been apart too long and the connection between them was weaker, but it was still there. He noticed her copper hair was loose tonight, falling to her shoulders in soft curls. She rarely wore a dress, but her denim skirt was short and her legs bare. Strappy sandals showed off her slender feet and painted toenails. He thought she looked stunning.

She saw him at almost the same instant and managed a tentative smile. Not scared exactly, he thought, but definitely apprehensive. This should be an interesting evening. 'I got you a beer. That OK?'

She nodded and slipped into the seat opposite him, slightly out of breath, so he guessed she'd walked. She picked up the glass and made wet rings on the table for a moment, then she met his eyes and sighed.

'I'm sorry, Noel. I never really thanked you, and I know I have a lot to thank you for, but I don't like things I don't understand. My mother is quite enough. I don't need any more strange things in my life.'

He laughed. 'I've been called a few names in my time, but never a strange thing. That's a first.' When she went to speak, he reached across the table and pressed a finger to her lips to shush her. 'Forget the past, Cass. Tell me what you want to see me about tonight.' He felt a little tingle of pleasure when he removed his finger and saw her lick her lips, but he listened in silence while she ran through the visit from Rachel and her examination of the stones.

'So they're real?'

'I think so. No, I'm positive. Besides, if they were fakes they would be worth nearly as much as the real thing. They're that good.'

'I didn't think sapphires were particularly valuable. Not like diamonds.'

'Good ones are. These sapphires are big and, as far as I can tell, near perfect.'

'Hide in plain sight,' he said thoughtfully. 'Clever.'

'You should have seen the setting they were stuck on.' She shuddered. 'It was horrendous.'

He closed his eyes. 'You threw it away, didn't you?'

When he opened his eyes again she was frowning at him. 'The bits of metal are in my safe. I'm not stupid, Noel.'

No, she wasn't. He should have remembered that. And if she said the stones were real, then they were real. She had an affinity with gemstones, a kind of rapport that he had never witnessed before. But then there were a lot of things he had never witnessed before — not until he met Cassandra Moon.

'How many people have you told so far?'

'You and my mother.'

'Keep it that way for the time being.

There may be an explanation that makes everything legal, but I can't think of one. Don't say anything about the stones being real sapphires to this Rachel person. At the moment she doesn't know exactly what she brought through customs, and what she doesn't know should keep her safe.'

'How about Liz? She's bound to ask me about the necklace. She works with Rachel.'

'Tell Liz the truth. You've managed to clean up the stones and you're going to reset them. That should be enough of the truth to keep her happy.'

He watched, fascinated, as Cass worked through the implications of keeping quiet. She rarely did anything impulsively and he could practically see the cogs turning.

'What happens if the man who gave Rachel the stones gets in touch with her? What if he comes with her to pick up the finished necklace? If he knows the stones are real, it won't take him long to figure out that I know as well.

He'll probably kill us both on the spot and throw our bodies in the river.'

'A distinct possibility, I agree. But I intend to make sure that doesn't happen. How long before you finish the new necklace?'

'I've got to do some drawings first. Different settings for the stones. That will take me to the end of next week because I've got some other work to finish. I can make an appointment for Rachel to view the drawings on Thursday or Friday.'

'Great. At the moment we don't know what we're dealing with. The boyfriend might just be a pawn, completely ignorant of what's going on; but if he is, then he knows the next person up in the chain, and that's who we want.' He reached across and took her glass. 'Another beer?'

'You aren't driving, I take it?'

He shook his head. 'I'll get a taxi. I can get the driver to drop you off, if you like.' He waved the glass at her. 'Same again?' Without giving her a chance to answer he headed for the bar. Now he'd got her in front of him he didn't intend to let her go just yet. He'd felt a change in the air since meeting Cassandra Moon for the first time, as if he were on the verge of something extraordinary. Something magical. He needed answers, and Cassandra and her mother held the key. He turned to look at her as he reached the bar, saw her watching him and smiled. He knew she could feel it too, that ethereal cord that bound them together, and one day she would be forced to admit it. For the moment he was prepared to wait. He thought she might relax over her second drink. Business was out of the way and they were just two acquaintances meeting for a beer, but she seemed even more wound up. A coiled spring waiting to unravel at any moment.

'I need to get home,' she said suddenly.

He frowned as she put her glass, still half-full, back on the table and got to her feet. He caught her by the wrist, feeling the tension in her arm, and a fizz of electrical energy.

'See!' She pulled her hand free. 'You can feel it, too, can't you?'

'Sit down, Cass.' He said it firmly, talking to her as he might to a suspect in the interview room back at the police station. 'You can't run away from it any more than I can. So sit down and let's talk it through.' He waited until she grudgingly sank back on to her chair. 'You don't believe in the supernatural. OK. In that case let's take a scientific approach. When we're together we both feel an electrical current of some sort. Very mild most of the time, like now, but strong enough to wake the dead when necessary.'

She gave him a reluctant smile. 'I wasn't dead.'

'Maybe not, but your heart had stopped, and that's the same thing to me.' He reached across the table and rested his hand on hers. 'See? There's nothing to be afraid of.

'I'm not afraid. I don't understand it,

but I'm not afraid of it.' She pulled a face. 'Well, maybe a little.'

He kept hold of her hand. 'I checked on Google for similar effects and I discovered that we all have electricity in our bodies. Some people are so conductive they can make a light bulb glow, and there is an eel that can give you an electric shock. Electricity is everywhere, Cass. You only have to look at lightening. Electricity from the sky powerful enough to kill. I don't know why we feel it sometimes when we're close, but you can't keep away from me. You need me. Like now, for instance.'

He let go of her hand and watched her pick up her drink. He hadn't fooled her, he knew that. This wasn't about police business, this went much deeper.

Cass stared at him for a few seconds and then she sighed resignedly. 'OK. So now what? What's the plan? What do we do about the necklace?'

Straight back to business. That was fine with him. Better than having her walk out on him. 'Carry on as normal

— as if the stones were just blue glass. Do your drawings for Rachel like you promised, but let me know when she's coming to look at them, and I'll be there too.' He almost laughed at the look of shock on her face. 'There's no need for Rachel to know I'm a policeman. I'll pretend to be your boyfriend.'

'That won't work.'

'Yes it will. Trust me. As you already know, I'm a very good actor when I need to be.' He took his phone out of his pocket. 'Drink up. I'd better get you home before your mother thinks we've eloped together.'

★ ★ ★

Just for one moment, one very small moment, Cass let her imagination wander. Eloping with Noel would be exciting, to say the least. Electrifying might be a better word. But he was right. In spite of what her mother would have them believe, there was nothing supernatural in a slight tingle occasionally when they touched one another. She got the same sensation from an inanimate object if it was full of static electricity. Well, almost the same sensation.

The cab driver took them to the end of the short drive that led up to the house.

'I'll stop here mate, if it's all the same to you. I might not be able to turn round up there.'

Cass was about to tell him there was a turning circle in front of the house, but then she realised it had nothing to do with turning the cab around. Her mother was a witch, and everybody knew it.

Noel told the taxi to wait and came round to open her door. 'I'll walk you to your gate.'

The moon was almost full, painting the front of the old house with silver and turning her mother's Japanese maple into something magical. The smell of night-scented jasmine hung heavy in the air and cicadas hummed in a nearby field. Cass was about to open the gate into the front garden when something touched her leg. A small black cat was rubbing round her ankles. She felt the seductive brush of soft fur against her bare skin and the vibration of a purr. She was about to bend down and stroke it when she noticed Noel had backed away. He looked as if he had just spotted a hooded cobra in mid-strike.

'Don't you like cats?' she asked in surprise.

'I'm allergic. Have been for as long as I can remember. It's the fur; it brings me out in a rash.'

She looked at him curiously. He was breathing heavily and there was a film of sweat on his brow. Not the reaction of someone afraid of an allergic rash — more like someone face to face with one of his worst fears.

She unlatched the gate. 'You go through first. I'll stop it following us in.'

Worried the cat might try to slip past her, she picked it up and held it in her arms. She wasn't quite sure what happened next. The small, furry creature that had been happily rubbing round her legs turned into something composed mainly of teeth and claws. The cat was either completely feral or terrified of being held. Probably both, she decided, as it tried to bite her hand down to the bone.

Cass threw the hissing, spitting animal away from her, but not before it had ripped a claw down her arm and sunk its teeth into the palm of her hand. Noel caught her wrist and dragged her through the gate, slamming it shut. The cat stared at them for a moment with slitted green eyes, back arched and teeth bared, before it disappeared into the darkness. Shaking, she put a hand over her bleeding arm and tried not to sob at the pain in her hand.

'That's why I don't like cats,' Noel said gruffly. 'How badly did it hurt you?' When she didn't answer, he put his arm round her waist. 'Let's get you inside. Dora will know what to do.'

For once, Cass was glad to see her mother waiting at the door.

'What happened?'

'A cat,' Noel said. 'I think it scratched Cass pretty badly.'

Dora looked past him at the moonlit garden. 'You didn't let it in, did you?'

Cass shook herself free from Noel's protective arm and walked ahead of him into the kitchen. 'I'm fine. It's a cat scratch, that's all.' She let Dora look at the wound and was surprised at the extent of the damage. The cat had gouged a deep furrow in her arm that ran from inside her elbow nearly to her wrist. She saw her mother press her lips together, her eyes simmering with anger.

'Where else? Where else did it hurt you?'

Cass held out her hand. The cat had made a puncture wound, already swollen and turning blue, on the fleshy mound at the base of her thumb. The initial fierce pain had subsided, leaving a dull ache. Right that moment she felt anything *but* fine. Her arm felt as if it was on fire and her hand throbbed like a bad tooth. She closed her eyes and hoped she didn't pass out.

'Your hand is already infected,' Dora said. 'If both of you sit down I'll do my best to fix it.' She opened a cupboard, took down a small bottle, and tipped pale green fluid into a glass. 'Drink this. I'll mix up something for you to soak your hand in.'

Cass looked at the glass suspiciously. The stuff was swirling around as if it had a life of its own. 'What is it?'

'Just herbs. Don't be such a baby.' Dora already had a large plastic bowl half full of warm water on the counter. 'I'm going into my office to find what I need.' She looked at Noel. 'Make her drink that potion. I don't know what that cat has infected her with, but we need to stop it in its tracks.'

As her mother left the room, Cass picked up the glass. 'It's OK. You don't have to hold my nose and force it down me. I'll drink it.' She took a sip and pulled a face. The stuff tasted like raw spinach mixed with vodka, which it probably was, unless it was chopped-up mandrake root. Knowing her mother, it could be just about anything. She swallowed the rest and put the glass back on the table.

'So, what is it with you and cats? I don't buy the allergy story. Just for a moment there, you looked terrified.'

'And so he should,' Dora said, as she came back into the room. 'All birds are scared of cats. It's a survival instinct.'

'His surname may be Raven, but he's not a bird, Mother. He's a police detective. He's not supposed to be afraid of anything. Particularly not a fluffy little kitten.'

Dora caught hold of Cass's wrist and pulled her arm out straight, exposing the length of the wound. Still wet with fresh blood, it looked more like a surgical incision than a cat scratch.

Noel hissed breath in through his teeth. 'That's a nasty-looking injury, considering it came from a fluffy little kitty.'

Dora humphed. 'You should listen to him, Cassie. If you lose your arm due to infection perhaps you'll be more careful next time. Besides, you should have realised that was no ordinary house cat.'

'No one has mentioned a feral cat being loose anywhere in Norton.' Cass winced as her mother added something to the water out of a pipette and pushed her hand into the bowl. The liquid was now an astringent yellow with strange black flecks floating in it, but it dulled the pain a little. 'Besides, the cat was behaving quite normally until I picked it up.'

'It was desperate to get through the gate,' Noel said quietly. He looked at Dora questioningly. 'Why was that, I wonder?'

Cass closed her eyes and pressed a finger against the bridge of her nose. She was starting to get a headache. 'Because it had to be invited inside,' she said, before her mother could reply. 'And if we'd spoken to it, or held the gate open for it, it would have been the same as giving it an invitation.'

Noel frowned at her. 'You would have let it in if it hadn't bitten you, wouldn't you?'

'Probably.' She scowled at him. 'I know all the myths and legends, but that doesn't mean I believe in them.' She was tired and she wanted to go to bed. 'When I bent down to stroke a small black cat, I wasn't expecting it to turn into a vampire or werewolf or whatever. I still think it was just a scared little pussy cat, but I'm obviously in the minority.'

'One day that attitude will get you killed, Cassie,' Dora said. 'You need to take more care.'

Cass lifted her hand out of the bowl and let her mother dab it dry. She always finished up feeling guilty. She knew her mother worried about her. Cass had thought her father was dead until a few months ago, but knowing he

41

was alive didn't make much difference; they were still two women living alone together in a big old house.

'I'm sorry. I didn't mean to sound ungrateful. I'm just tired, I think.'

Noel stood up. 'I must go. The cab's waiting at the end of the drive.'

Dora picked up the bowl and tipped the remaining liquid down the sink. 'The drivers won't come right up to the house. They've heard I'm a witch.' She tutted with disgust. 'You'd think I was a hobgoblin or something.'

Because you post information about being a witch all over Facebook, Mother, Cass thought. The notoriety might help her mother's business, but it played hell with their social life.

'I'll walk you to the gate,' she said to Noel. 'Just in case the cat's still hanging around.'

If it was, she would do her good deed for the day and scare it away, but this time she'd try throwing rocks at it.

3

Cass heard the knock on her studio door just as she was shutting up for the day, and guessed it must be Liz. She knew she would have to speak to Liz about the necklace eventually. She hoped Liz didn't ask any direct questions she couldn't answer, because she hated lying.

'Did Rachel come to see you?' Liz asked, almost before she was through the door. 'I hope it wasn't a nuisance for you. She showed me the broken necklace, and the stones were so pretty I told her you could probably mend it for her. I know she can afford it; she's just been left some money.'

'It's fine. I can't mend it, so I suggested she have the stones reset. I'm doing some drawings for her. I thought I might put three of the stones in a necklace and set the other two as matching earrings.'

'Oh, that sounds great. Thanks, Cass. She was so disappointed about the guy she met not coming back to England with her, I thought you might be able to cheer her up. I haven't seen her since I gave her your name. You know what the hospital is like. We pass one another like fish in the dark.'

'I think it should be ships in the night, but fish will do. I'll phone Rachel tomorrow and tell her the drawings are ready.' Cass opened a drawer and took out three sheets of A4 paper. 'What do you think?'

'Wow! Can you really make those blue beads look this good?' She picked up the design Cass already felt would work the best. 'This is the one I'd choose. It's amazing. Even if the guy never shows up again, she'll have something to remind her of a nice holiday romance. Thanks, Cass.'

'No problem.' Cass felt the beginnings of a squirm coming on and changed the subject the best way she knew how. 'You walked here, didn't you? So how about a glass of cold Chardonnay? I know my mother has some in her fridge, and she always likes to talk to you when you come round.'

Liz grinned. 'What are we waiting for?'

Cass was glad to lock up her studio and head into the house. She knew Noel had been right not to worry Liz before they knew anything definite, but she felt bad about keeping secrets from her friend. She had known Liz for years, from the time she first worked on the front desk at the hospital. She had left the hospital when her jewellery business started to earn proper money, but the two women still remained close friends.

Liz had coffee-coloured skin and dark brown hair that matched her eyes, and usually wore her short hair in carefully waxed spikes. Today she was wearing a bright red skirt that just covered her knees, a black sleeveless top with a deep V-neck and flat sandals.

Very modest attire for Liz; she was usually more adventurous.

The French doors to the patio were open and Dora had a chilled bottle of Chardonnay ready on the kitchen table. Cass never asked her mother how she did that. She didn't want to know the answer.

They took their drinks outside on to the little patio and sat in the dappled shade of another large Japanese acer. Cass found herself checking to make sure no cats had got into the garden. She was wearing a thin top with long sleeves to hide the scar on her arm. The wound was healing nicely, thanks to her mother, but Cass found it embarrassing. A cat scratch wasn't the most noble of wounds. The puncture in the palm of her hand was hardly noticeable, but it was taking longer to heal and still kept her awake at night. She had refused the offer of something to help her sleep. She had once been foolish enough to try her mother's homemade sedative, probably made with the notorious mandrake, and hadn't woken up for two days.

The sun was setting and the shadows were lengthening. Cass had been feeling edgy ever since the incident with the cat. Anything could be hiding in the deep undergrowth. For all her bravado, she knew the cat had attacked out of anger rather than fear. She had seen the look in those slanting green eyes before it ran off into the night. Malevolent was the best word she could come up with, and she wished she hadn't come up with that one.

She had been fine before Noel Raven appeared on the scene. He had brought something strange into her life, something she didn't understand, and she wished he'd go away and take whatever it was with him. It was bad enough having her mother going on all the time about magic potions and witchcraft without Noel egging her on.

'Have you heard anything about a feral cat in the area?' she asked Liz. She wondered if anyone else had been

47

injured. If so, they would probably finish up in the hospital.

Liz shook her head. 'Why?'

'Cass got attacked outside the house by a cat,' Dora said. 'It clawed her arm and made a hole in her hand.'

Liz looked at Cass reproachfully. 'You didn't say anything to me. Why didn't you say anything?'

'Because it's all healed up.' She sometimes wished her mother would keep her mouth shut, but that was never going to happen. 'My little witch mother slapped some goo on it, and it's just fine.'

'Let me see.' Liz pulled up Cass's sleeve and gave a little gasp of horror. 'It must have been some scratch.' She looked at the dark bushes edging the patio. 'What happened to the cat? Where did it go?'

'It can't get in,' Dora said.

Liz didn't look convinced. 'Cats can get in most places.'

'Not in here.' Dora filled their glasses. 'The house and gardens are protected.'

'Noel Raven doesn't like cats,' Cass

volunteered. She wanted to change the subject before Liz could ask what sort of protection her mother was talking about. It certainly wasn't a burglar alarm. 'He has an allergy or something.'

Liz shuddered. 'Having seen that scratch on your arm, I'm not surprised. I'm definitely allergic to anything that can do that sort of damage. Do you think it'll attack anyone else?'

Dora shook her head. 'It wanted to get in here. Into the house. I don't think it was after Noel. I don't think it knows what he is.'

Cass gave her mother a warning look. 'He's a policeman, Mother. Besides, the cat attacked me.'

'Because it thought you were going to let it into our garden, and it got annoyed when you tried to stop it. Perhaps you'll be more careful next time.'

Cass didn't want to think about a next time. The cat had scared her more than she cared to admit. The change from a dear little moggy into something lethally feral had been too sudden. Unnaturally sudden. But her mother didn't have to worry. The pain in her hand had been enough to put her off anything remotely feline for a long time.

Dora asked Liz to stay for dinner, but she refused. 'I have to get back home and get some sleep. I'm on the early shift tomorrow.'

Cass said goodbye to her friend and helped her mother set the table. They always sat in the kitchen for the evening meal, and tonight Dora kept the doors open to let in the cool evening air. She had set out tumblers, and was just filling a jug with her mother's home-made lemonade when Noel appeared on the patio.

'Sorry,' he said. 'You're about to eat. I just wanted to check on your cat scratches, Cass. Are you all healed up?'

'Noel! How lovely to see you.' Dora turned from the stove where she had been checking something in a sauce-pan. 'Have you come straight from work?' When he nodded, she grabbed another placemat and set it on the table. 'I've made a light summer stew. Chicken and herbs. Please stay for dinner. If you don't I shall have to freeze half of it.'

Noel looked at Cass as if asking her approval, and she shrugged her shoulders. 'Don't look at me. As far as I'm concerned you're welcome to stay if you haven't got anywhere more pressing to go.' She pushed up her sleeve. 'My arm is healing nicely and I still have the use of my thumb.' It scared her when she thought how much it would have affected her work if her hand had been permanently damaged.

'No more sightings of the murderous cat, then? I thought someone else might have seen it, or at least had a run-in with it, so I asked around, but I got nothing back from anyone. Not even any half-eaten rats or mice lying around.'

'They wouldn't have been half-eaten,' Cass muttered, as she set an extra place at the table.

Noel took the cold beer Dora handed him. 'Thanks Dora. I'm surprised you haven't got a cat of your own. Aren't witches supposed to have a familiar?'

'I had a cat before Cassie was born,' Dora said, 'but she was too gentle. I should have trained her better.'

Cass knew nothing about her mother having had a cat. Dora had never mentioned having any sort of pet. 'What happened to it?' she asked curiously.

'The poor little thing was killed. She happened to be in the wrong place at the wrong time, and didn't know how to defend herself. Like I said, I should have trained her better. Would you like a beer, Cassie? Or do you want another glass of wine?'

Cass knew her mother wouldn't talk any more about the cat — once Dora changed the subject, that was it — but now she was curious. Noel was right — if Dora was so convinced she was a witch, why didn't she have a cat? Still thinking about it, Cass said no to the offer of more alcohol and filled a tall glass with soda water.

'Should we get a cat?' she asked her mother. 'Would you like another one?'

Dora shook her head. 'I'd be afraid I wouldn't be able to keep it safe.' She turned to Noel. 'Have you found out any more about our smuggling ring? Cass has finished the drawings for the woman with the sapphires.'

'When is she coming to look at them?' Noel ignored the empty glass Dora had put in front of him and drank his beer straight from the bottle.

'I don't know; I haven't contacted her yet.' Cass watched him down half the bottle of beer in one go. There was something very masculine about Noel Raven — it was present in everything he did; so his reaction to the feral cat had been completely out of character. She supposed everyone had their Achilles heel, but it had shocked her all the same.

'I need to be there, Cass. I want to meet this woman and make up my own mind about her. She may be in serious danger from the man who gave her the necklace, or she may be his accomplice. Either way, I don't want you to see her on your own.'

He was throwing his weight around again, and it was on the tip of Cass's tongue to make a sarcastic remark, but she was the one who had asked for his help so it was only fair to let him do his job. 'I'll tell you when she's coming to see me, but I don't think the boyfriend thing will work. Can't you be a customer or something?'

'I can hardly take an interest in the woman's necklace and ask questions if I'm just a customer, can I? It would be none of my business. But if I'm your lover . . . '

'Hold on a minute. You were going to be my boyfriend originally, and I haven't agreed to that yet, so when did you suddenly become my lover?'

'Natural progression of events,' Noel said innocently, barely suppressing a grin. 'We've been together for so long it would be strange if we weren't sleeping together by now.'

'In your dreams, Noel Raven!'

Cass was about to protest further, but her mother put a casserole dish of chicken stew on the table and Noel pulled out a chair for her.

'Don't get your knickers in a twist, Cass. It's all make-believe. And besides, you know I can't get too close to you. If we really were lovers, I'd probably disappear in a sudden flash of lightening.'

'Let the stones talk to you, Cassie,' Dora said enigmatically as she dished up the stew. 'And listen to what they say. Sapphires are all about honesty and clarity of vision — and the sapphire is your birthstone.'

Noel looked up from his plate. 'The sapphire is September, isn't it? So your birthday must be sometime soon.'

'Yeah,' Cass said. 'Sometime soon.' She knew she was being deliberately perverse. The detective already knew far too much about her. More than her best friend, Liz. Now he wanted to know how old she was.

'I didn't ask your age,' Noel said, as if reading her thoughts. 'Even though I know exactly how old you are. I just asked when your next birthday is due. But I can look that up as well if you don't want to tell me. I was just making polite conversation.' He picked up his knife and fork. 'However, I'd much rather eat this delicious stew, so forget I even spoke.'

Dora laughed. 'When you two get together you're worse than a couple of kids. Eat your dinner, Cassie. It might put you in a better mood.'

Cass could remember those exact words from her childhood. She *was* behaving like a spoiled child, and she had no idea why. Noel Raven seemed to bring out the worst in her. Maybe because she fancied him like mad and he obviously didn't feel the same way about her. With Noel, it was all about the job. He was here now, in her house, eating her mother's food, because he wanted to catch a smuggler. It had nothing to do with concern about her cat bite.

Noel mopped up his gravy with a piece of bread, something Cass had been told she must never do because it was unladylike, but now Dora was watching Noel with a pleased smile on her face.

The detective refused the offer of coffee, saying he had to call in at the police station on his way back. 'Let me know when you arrange a meeting with Rachel Saunders,' he said to Cass. 'Give me a day's notice if you can, so I can change my schedule if necessary. I really want to meet the woman.'

'I'm not going to lie to her, Noel.'

He stopped on his way to the door. 'You don't have to. You said you were going to show her some drawings, and you are. Just don't volunteer any information.'

'I'm not going to tell her you're my boyfriend.'

'I could be. Then you wouldn't have to lie.'

He was smiling at her: a tall man

with silver-grey eyes and thick black hair. He had a day's growth of stubble on his face and a spot of chicken stew on his shirt — and he looked as sexy as hell. The desire to touch him was almost overwhelming.

Cass mentally cursed herself. Stupid! She was being stupid. But as she looked at him everything seemed to slow down and she felt the familiar tingle in the tips of her fingers. Dora said something, but her words were slurred. Cass felt lightheaded and her head started to swim, but she wasn't going to faint. She definitely wasn't going to faint. Not this time. She could control this — she had to learn how to control it — or behave like a fool every time she was anywhere near Noel Raven.

He took a step forward, but Dora held up her hand.

'Wait, Noel, don't touch her. Cassie, are you all right? You look as if you've seen a ghost.'

Cass gave herself a mental shake and felt her head clear. 'I don't know what you're talking about, Mother. I'm fine. And Noel has to go. He has to get back to the police station.'

'You may be fine now, Cassie, but if this has happened before, we need to get to the bottom of it.'

Noel looked at her curiously. 'It has happened before, hasn't it, Cass? We both know that. What do you think triggered it this time?'

Cass felt both sets of eyes on her and the heat rose to her face. 'I have no idea. I just felt a little odd for a moment, but I'm fine now.' She looked at her mother as if daring her to say anything. 'Probably something I ate.'

'If you think that was stomach upset, you're not as bright as I thought you were,' Dora said crossly. 'Besides, there was nothing wrong with my stew.'

Noel made his way to the door again and this time he opened it. 'Cass is right, I have to go. Take care of her, Dora.'

Cass waited until he shut the door before she turned on her mother. 'You know why this happens to me, don't you? I need you to tell me. An answer I can understand, not some magical gobbledygook.'

Dora sighed. 'The only answer I can give you will be magical gobbledygook. Leave it for now, Cassie. We're both tired. Give me time to speak to someone who knows more than I do, and then I may be able to help you. In the meantime I'm going to see about getting another cat. I think we might need one.'

★   ★   ★

Dora went into her office as soon as Cassandra disappeared upstairs to bed. She needed to compose an email to her husband, a task she hated, but she couldn't contact him any other way. She had no idea where he was at any given time. He might be on a special mission somewhere, but that some-where could be anywhere in the world. He could be on a plane, or a ship, or a train. He might be in Hawaii, or at a hotel down the road. She knew he had a mobile phone, but he never answered it. Hector Moon was an enigma, never what he seemed. He rarely used his real name and could disappear on a whim, eventually emerging as a completely different person in an entirely different place.

She thought carefully about her email. She needed to attract his attention, otherwise he would ignore her. She clicked on 'new' and stared at the screen for a while. Nothing was easy anymore, but if she kept her email brief, he might at least read it.

I need a cat, Hector. Not a female this time. A strong male. Something is trying to get into the house and Cassandra almost let it in. When she didn't, it hurt her. She doesn't understand her power and she can't handle it. She needs help.

And so did she, Dora thought ruefully, but she wasn't going to tell

Hector that. While she was waiting for his reply, she took a bottle of wine out of her little refrigerator and poured herself a generous glassful. She looked at it thoughtfully for a moment and then added a drop of something from a bottle on her apothecary shelf. She needed a jolt of something strong.

His email, when it eventually arrived, was as brief as hers.

> *You can't have a male cat, Pandora. You are a woman. I will make enquiries about a suitable feline and get back to you. I think I should meet with my daughter.*

Pandora sat back in her chair so hard it shot across the room on its wheels and banged into the wall. Hector had never even hinted at meeting Cassandra until today. So what had changed?

She stared at the computer screen in frustration. She needed to speak to her husband, not communicate by email. She hadn't actually spoken to Hector for several years. She might not even recognise his voice anymore. Once she had loved him; now she wasn't so sure.

For the first time Dora felt scared. From the moment Cassandra had been born she had wanted her to meet her father, but he had said Cassandra was still vulnerable, and keeping away was what kept her safe. Now he was willing to meet her. So what had changed? Dora asked herself again, even though she already knew the answer.

The only thing that was different was the arrival of Noel Raven.

4

Rachel phoned the next day and Cass made an appointment to show her the drawings the following Friday. She considered not saying anything to Noel about Rachel's visit — her business arrangements were nothing to do with him — but she knew he would find out. He was a detective, after all. The whole idea of him pretending to be her boyfriend was ridiculous, but she had protection of a sort. If he tried to get too close to her he would probably disappear in a flash of lightening.

She had a nasty suspicion he intended to use Rachel as bait to smoke out the smugglers, and she wished she had just reset the stones and handed them back, but it was too late now. Hopefully the guy who had given Rachel the necklace would never be seen again, which would solve most of their problems. There was no way Noel could track him down, because it was unlikely Rachel even knew his last name, and Cass knew she didn't have an address for him.

So why, she asked herself, was she standing in front of her mirror wondering what to wear? Why did it matter? Jeans and a T-shirt was her usual working attire, but for some reason she was holding a dress that she hadn't worn for months, and seriously considering a pair of shoes with heels. She slipped on the dress, having decided any girl would want to look her best if she were meeting her boyfriend, but swapped the heels for a pair of flat sandals. There was no need to go overboard. She tied her unruly hair off her face in a loose ponytail, hoping it looked more business-like than sexy, and chose a pair of modest pearl studs for her ears. She never tried to advertise her jewellery by wearing it herself, a practice she found a little pretentious.

Noel arrived half an hour before

Rachel, letting himself in the back door of the house. He greeted Dora with a kiss on the cheek and told her she was looking radiant. When she looked at him in surprise, he laughed. 'I'm your daughter's boyfriend for the day, so I'm getting into character. Besides, you always look lovely, Dora.' He turned to Cassandra and gave a low whistle. 'Wow, a dress. I'm feeling quite honoured.'

'You've seen me in a dress before,' Cass said impatiently. 'And this isn't for you, so don't get ideas. I'm just going along with your charade.'

Dora tutted. 'Oh, get rid of that stick up your bottom, Cassie, and enjoy yourself. It's play-acting, something you used to be good at.' She turned to Noel. 'Cassie played Juliet in the school play. Her drama teacher wanted her to go on to acting school. Do you remember, Cassie?'

Cass remembered all too well. For that hour on the stage she had lost herself in the part. For a little while she was a beautiful child, worshipped by her teenage lover, but then he died, and she cried real tears, sobbing on the stage in front of her classmates. She desperately wanted to stay in that world of make-believe, but she discovered reality was out there waiting to humiliate her. She could still remember the embarrassment of having to stand up in front of everyone and listen to the applause, her heart broken and the tears still wet on her face. She never volunteered to be in a school play again. It hurt too much.

Now she looked at Noel and tried to work out what it was about him that got under her skin. It wasn't really his fault that he was tall, dark, good-looking and sexy. Although he could try playing it down a little. Today he was wearing jeans that were almost indecently tight and a pale grey shirt that matched his eyes. The top two buttons were undone, something she considered completely unnecessary.

'We ought to go to the studio,' she

said. 'Rachel is due in ten minutes and she might be early.'

Cass saw Noel wink at her mother as he left the kitchen, and that really annoyed her.

When they got to the studio she took the bag holding the sapphires out of her safe and tipped them onto a square of black velvet on her workbench. As Noel leant over for a closer look, the stones gleamed with a life of their own.

'Beautiful,' he said. 'Can I pick them up?'

'Of course. They won't bite you. The gems look good cleaned and polished, don't they?'

Noel took the round sapphire and held it in the centre of his palm. 'What are you going to do with this?'

Cass unrolled her drawings and flattened them out beside the stones. 'I've made the drawings to scale. If you put the one you're holding in the centre — that's it, right in the middle — the other two will go on either side. The smaller two will make a pair of matching earrings.'

He moved the stones around on her drawings as if he were doing some sort of puzzle. She watched him, amused, but secretly glad he was interested in her work.

'I like this drawing best. What are you going to use for the setting?'

'I can do that particular design myself using gold wire, so I hope she chooses that one. I have a friend with a kiln who can help me with the other two designs.'

They were so intent on the drawings that the knock on the door made them both jump. Cass looked at Noel, nerves cramping her stomach.

'Just play it by ear,' he said soothingly. 'Being my girlfriend for a day can't be that bad, surely.'

That made her smile, and she opened the door with the smile still on her face. She didn't intend to tell a direct lie, but hopefully she wouldn't have to. Noel would be the one asking any awkward questions.

Rachel was by herself; that was the first hurdle out of the way. She looked as nervous as Cass felt, her eyes darting to Noel.

'You have company. Shall I come back some other time?'

Noel stepped forward and held out his hand. 'Sorry. I came round to see Cass and she said I could stay. She let me have a quick look at her designs and I think you'll like them. Your little blue stones look great now she's cleaned them up.'

Not lying, Cass thought. *Just bending the truth. Clever.* He could be anyone — friend, lover, jewellery buff, or just a nosy neighbour. He was letting Rachel draw her own conclusion.

'We've already been playing with the designs,' Cass said. 'You can lay the stones on the drawings in any order you like. If you don't like any of the designs, just say so. I can make any changes you like.'

Rachel walked over to the workbench. 'Wow,' she said solemnly, a touch of awe in her voice. 'The stones look so different. Are you sure they're the same ones I gave you? These are beautiful.'

Cass ignored the implication that she might have substituted the stones she had been given for something else. She knew Rachel didn't mean it the way it sounded, and she could understand the woman's surprise. Although Rachel didn't know it, she was looking at several thousand pounds' worth of top-grade sapphires. They had a right to look beautiful.

Noel opened Cass's refrigerator and took out three bottles of beer. He held one out to Rachel and she took it with a smile. 'I didn't drive here, so I can have a beer. I caught the bus. You can have as many as you like; Cass won't mind. We've known one another a long time.'

That was the first lie of the day, Cass thought. She'd met Noel for the first time three months ago, and that didn't count as a long time as far as she was concerned. Rachel couldn't take her eyes off him, and Cass found that irritating. If he really had been her boyfriend, it would have been bordering on rude.

She had been watching Rachel shuffle the stones around, but now she looked up from the table and caught Noel's eye. He smiled at her, and she felt the familiar tingle. She shook her head, not knowing if he understood her warning. Shooting sparks at one another in front of Rachel might not be a good idea.

'Oh!' Rachel exclaimed suddenly, pulling her hand away. 'I think I got a shock from one of the stones. Can that happen?'

Around here it can, Cass thought as she moved to the table. She picked up one of the sapphires and nearly dropped it. It was icy cold. So cold it stuck to her fingers and she thought she might have freezer burn. She forced herself to keep hold of the stone and smile at Rachel.

'It's just cold. It must have been lying against your bottle of beer.' She rubbed the offending sapphire with a cloth and felt the cold disperse, then handed it back to Rachel. 'See? It's fine now.'

Rachel took the stone gingerly and Cass hoped she hadn't lost the sale. If Rachel went home with the sapphires she would be arrested; Noel would see to that. He was looking at Cass curiously, not sure what had just happened, and there was no way she was going to enlighten him. The sapphire is all about emotion, and Cass had a nasty feeling she might have caused the odd reaction in the stone. She had been thinking about Noel, and watching Rachel eyeing him up, and although the thought horrified her she might have been feeling slightly jealous. Earlier in the year she had nearly killed a woman with a red-hot ruby, so an ice-cold sapphire wasn't that surprising. The stones were just trying to protect her.

'I like this one best,' Rachel said, holding up the drawing Cass hoped she'd choose. 'It's really simple, but I think it'll show my pretty stones off best. They don't need a lot of fancy stuff round them, do they? That was what was wrong before. How long will it take to do the setting?'

'Two or three weeks, probably. The design may look simple, but it takes a long time and a lot of patience to work the wire. Do you want the earrings as drops or studs?'

'Drops, please, and I need to know how much it's all going to cost.'

'I can only give you a rough idea because I'm not sure how long it will take to finish the pieces.' She named a price Rachel seemed happy with. 'Have you heard from the guy who gave you the necklace? I wondered if he was back in England yet.'

Rachel shook her head. 'I have no idea where he is. I told you I won't see him again. It's a pity, because I'd like to show him the necklace when it's finished. He's never going to know how nice the stones look.'

'I agree. That will be a pity,' Noel said casually. 'Do you know his full name? You might be able to track him down online.'

Rachel shook her head again. 'It sounds awful, doesn't it, not knowing his last name, but we didn't sleep together or anything. I was hoping we could get to know one another better when we both got back to England, but perhaps he never intended to come back with me. Perhaps the sickness at the airport was just to get away from me.'

Cass thought it must be horrible to have such a poor opinion of yourself. Not that she'd done any better with men, but that was because she didn't want to get involved with anyone. Her life was complicated enough as it was without throwing anything else into the mix.

'I think he intended to come back with you,' Noel said. 'The man obviously cared about you. He came to the airport with you, and I presume he'd already bought a ticket back to England. He's probably still in hospital, or recuperating somewhere. Food poisoning can be nasty. I'm sure he'll be in touch. By the way — ' Noel made it sound like an afterthought. ' — do you know his first name?'

'Chris. Christopher, I suppose. He knows my last name because I told him, but I never asked his. I thought we were travelling back to England together and we'd have plenty of time to get to know those sort of things about one another. It's a long flight.'

And you had to do it all on your own, Cass thought. 'Let me know when he does contact you,' she said, 'because I know he will, and then we can show him what I'm planning to do with the necklace. I'm sure he'll be pleased.'

'Oh, he will. How could he not be?' Rachel took a last look at the stones on the bench. 'I can't believe they cleaned up so beautifully. I'm really looking forward to wearing them.'

Cass got her to sign the drawing she had chosen, then walked with her to the end of the drive. The road through the village was on a good bus route, so she wouldn't have to wait long for a bus.

When Cass got back inside the studio, Noel had already put the stones back in their bag and shut them in the safe. 'We didn't learn a lot,' he said. 'But I agree with you about Rachel being genuine. It would be nice to discover the boyfriend was innocent as well, but I very much doubt it. No one would have given him that necklace without very explicit instructions as to what to do with it when he got back to England. Rachel was being used to get the stones past customs. I've put in a request for a list of wanted items that might go through Miami airport, but customs officers move in exceedingly slow and mysterious ways, so it may take a while.'

'Talking of boyfriends,' she said, 'thank you for not pushing it.'

He raised an eyebrow. 'I wouldn't dare. If your mother thinks you could be dangerous, I'm certainly not taking any chances.'

She knew he was joking, but it still upset her. She didn't want him to be afraid of her. She didn't want anyone to be afraid of her. The damned sapphire had scared Rachel and nearly lost her a sale.

'What is it, Noel? What's happening to me? I don't like things I don't understand.' When she thought about it, she supposed it was only natural. As a child, she had learned to ignore things she didn't understand; *put it to one side and don't think about it* had been her motto. But now it was different, more personal, and she couldn't ignore the problem any longer. She had always had an affinity with gemstones, and loved working with them, but recently even her beloved stones had been behaving in a peculiar way.

Noel sat on the edge of her workbench and held out his hand. 'Hold my hand, Cass. It's safe at the moment. We'd both know if something was going to happen.'

She moved closer and took his hand. He was right: she knew exactly when danger lurked, and she knew exactly why. He obviously didn't. She tried to convince herself he was just a friend, almost like a brother, but she wasn't sure that sort of thinking would work. His hand was warm, and he had long fingers that closed around hers protectively. She pressed her lips together and mentally said her eight times table. She had always had a problem with that one.

'See?' he said, smiling into her eyes. 'Nothing to worry about. You can hold my hand whenever you feel like it.'

No, she couldn't. He had interrupted her school exercise, and that could be dangerous. She could feel the beginning of a tingle in her fingertips and tried to pull her hand away.

'Let me go, Noel.'

'No.' He looked at her curiously. 'What just changed? Something did. What were you thinking about?'

Flustered now, she tugged again at her hand. 'You,' she muttered almost inaudibly. 'I was thinking about you. Your hand felt nice; all warm and protective and — '

'Sexy,' he said softly. 'That's what

triggers it, isn't it?' He let go of her hand and stared at her in amazement. 'You actually fancy me.'

She felt humiliation rise like a hot red tide, starting at her toes and finishing up heating her face bright pink. 'Don't be ridiculous. It happens when I drop my guard and let you inside my defences.'

'And why would you do that, I wonder?'

He still had hold of her hand, his long fingers holding her fast. She pulled again, struggling to get her hand free from his. 'You have to let me go, Noel — I'm beginning to feel lightheaded again.' Actually she was feeling anything but lightheaded. The tingle in the tips of her fingers had coursed its way through the rest of her body and she felt charged up and ready for anything. Maybe they really were stronger together.

As she turned away, he pulled her round to face him. 'You don't feel lightheaded, do you, Cass? You feel invincible, like me. Ready to take on the rest of the world.' Before she could protest, he bent his head and touched his lips to hers.

She could have pulled away — maybe — but her lips had other ideas. There was nothing sexual in his kiss. He was carrying out an experiment, and they both knew it, but something extremely strange was happening all the same. She felt a surge of electricity as if she were plugged into a power socket — and then her feet left the floor. She would never be able to swear to it, she couldn't actually see a gap beneath her feet, but that was what it felt like. She remembered thinking the White Rabbit would appear any minute. Then Noel gently eased away from her and she found she had her mouth back.

He let go of her hand and slipped an arm round her waist as she staggered. 'Are you OK?'

'No, of course I'm not OK. Why did you do that? You knew what would happen.'

'No, I didn't know what would happen. We've been pussy-footing around this thing for several months, Cass, and I don't think we can ignore it any longer. Your mother is scared of something. Not you in particular, but something connected to you. You have some sort of . . . I don't know . . . call it a gift if you like, and maybe I do too. The thing is, neither of us know what to do with it, and I have a feeling we may need to use whatever power we have sometime fairly soon.'

She sank down on to her sofa after making sure her feet were firmly on the ground. 'Static electricity can be a bitch, can't it?' She smiled when she saw the look on his face. 'I know it was more than that, Noel, but it scares me. And we really don't have to deal with it. Not right now. Nothing will happen if we stay away from one another. You do your job and I'll do mine . . . '

'And never the twain shall meet? Do you really think that will work? Things will keep bringing us together, like your sapphire smuggler and the incident with the cat.'

'My mother is going to get her own cat,' she told him, moving to safer ground. 'Will that mean you can't come to the house? If you are allergic to cats you'll have to stay away, won't you?'

'I'm not allergic to cats, Cass, so don't get your hopes up. It was that particular cat. For some reason as soon as I saw it I wanted to run. I needed to get as far away from it as I could.'

'You were scared of it.'

'I was terrified of it.' He ran a hand through his hair, making it stand on end. 'The only time I've felt that bad was when I visited a prison and one of my mates thought it would be fun to lock me in a cell. I don't suffer from claustrophobia, but being shut in that cell terrified me.'

'You were shut in a cage, that's why it bothered you so much. Particularly if you go along with my mother's thinking. Birds don't like to be caged.' She thought for a moment. 'Have you ever jumped out of an aeroplane?'

He looked at her in surprise. 'No,

I've never jumped out of an aeroplane, but I did paraglide once. Why?'

'How did you feel?'

He grinned at her. 'Amazing. It was the best experience of my life. It was like being a . . . '

When he stopped, Cass smiled in triumph. 'Like being a bird, Noel. Is that what you were going to say?'

His grin faded. 'So what is it with me and birds? Apart from my name, I've certainly never thought about being a bird. I wanted to be a pilot once, a long time ago, but something to do with my peripheral vision meant I couldn't get a licence.'

'How about your parents?'

He shook his head. 'No idea. They were both killed in a car accident when I was ten. My grandmother took over the job of parenting. Looking after me should have worn her out, but she's still going strong in her mid-eighties.'

'So you don't remember much about your parents?' Cass saw the look on his face and stopped short. 'I'm sorry,

Noel. I didn't mean to interrogate you. I just wondered if there was anything at all in your past that would explain why we both behave like we do. I mean, it's obvious why I'm peculiar. I have a witch for a mother and a warlock for a father.'

He sat down beside her and she forced herself not to move away. 'You didn't tell me about the warlock. I'm not sure I know what one of those is.'

Cass could have kicked herself. What with storms and lightening, and electricity at her fingertips, she didn't need to give him any more ammunition to label her a freak. 'Google it,' she said, more sharply than she had intended. 'You know it's all part of my mother's silliness. If she's a witch, she thinks she ought to be married to a warlock. She makes it all up, Noel. She lives in a little fantasy world all her own.'

He put his hand over hers. 'Are you sure about that, Cassandra? What about us? The strange things that happen whenever we get together.'

She snatched her hand from under his, and this time she did move away, standing up before he could touch her again. 'It's static. You know it's static. You said so yourself.'

Noel Raven got to his feet, smiling when she moved further away. 'That was before I knew your father was a warlock.'

She held the door open for him. 'I'll let you know when the necklace is ready for collection.'

'And let me know when the new cat arrives. I think a big black raven should be a match for any itty-bitty pussycat. I'll just have to sharpen my beak.'

As Cass closed the door a tiny shiver moved down her spine, and she rubbed her arm. She had a nasty suspicion it would take more than a sharp beak to defeat one particular feline.

5

Christopher Dempsey sat on the side of his hospital bed and waited for the doctor. One last inspection to check he was well enough to travel, and then he was free to leave. All he had to do was pick up his suitcase and head back to the airport. He'd been in the hospital four days and lost half a stone. He had been seriously dehydrated, and for a little while he had thought he was going to die. Now all he wanted to do was get on a plane and fly back to England.

A nurse popped her head in the door. 'There's a guy here says he's come to take you to the airport.'

Chris got to his feet wondering if someone had ordered a cab for him, but the man who came through the door wasn't a cab driver. The man's name was Finchley. He was tall and heavily built, with a scar on his left cheek. The last time Chris had seen Finchley he had been wearing shorts, but today he was smartly dressed in a grey suit and carrying a briefcase.

He was the man who had given Chris a necklace on a Florida beach and offered him a large sum of money to take it out of the country.

'I heard you were taken ill,' Finchley said. 'I hope it didn't interfere with our little arrangement. I was getting worried about you.'

Chris shook his head. His heart was beating extra fast and his hands felt clammy. 'No. I did exactly what you told me.' If he was really lucky the nurse would come back and tell Finchley to leave. 'I'm flying back home today. I gave the woman the necklace and she took it back to England. She was wearing it when she got on the plane.'

'So where is it now?'

'She's still got it, but I know where she lives. She gave me her address. I've still got the replacement and I'll swap it as soon as I get back.' He looked hopefully at the door. 'The doctor will be here in a minute to sign me out.'

'Show me.'

Chris fumbled in his travel bag and took out a brown envelope, handing it to Finchley. Inside was a necklace with blue stones in a cheap silver-coloured setting. He could no longer remember what the original necklace looked like, but customs certainly wouldn't be interested in the one Finchley was holding in his hand.

'You were supposed to fly back with her. You shouldn't have let those stones out of your sight. That was part of the deal. You were supposed to keep an eye on the necklace at all times. Give me the woman's address. If *you* can't get the stones back, I know I can.'

Chris remembered the way Rachel had looked at him at the airport when he said he felt sick. She thought he was dumping her. He could see the hurt in her eyes. But he really had been sick. By the time he had staggered out of the restroom, she had already gone through the boarding gate. A few minutes later he collapsed and got rushed off to hospital. He really liked Rachel Saunders and he didn't want to give this man her address, but he did. He wrote it on a piece of paper, then handed it to him.

'Remember, I know where to find you, *and* I know where you work, so don't think of running off anywhere. You have a week to fly back to England, get back the original necklace, and pick up the other half of your payment. Otherwise, I'll pay the woman a visit myself.'

Chris barely had time to stuff the envelope back in his bag before a nurse walked into the room.

'I'm off,' the man said. 'See you in England, Chris.'

Chris felt sick again, but if he threw up now they wouldn't let him go home. He took a deep breath. All he had to do was swap the necklace and get the rest of his money, and then it would all be over. He might even be able to carry on seeing Rachel.

Noel got back to the police station and shut himself in his room. He didn't close the door very often because he liked to keep an eye on the outer office, but this time he wished his door had a lock.

He fired up his computer and stared at the screen. He had intended to check on his parentage, something he had never bothered to do before. His grandma had told him everything about his parents that she thought he needed to know, and it seemed disrespectful to start digging into his past at this late stage. If he had needed to know more, Myra Page would have told him. So instead he clicked on Google and typed in the word 'warlock'. He was surprised when so many sites popped up on his screen. He got boy bands, films and computer games, as well as numerous definitions: someone who practises black magic; a sorcerer, conjurer, enchanter and necromancer. So, according to the internet, a warlock seemed capable of anything from pulling a rabbit out of a hat to communing with the dead. Not someone he would want as a father-in-law, he decided, and then wondered where that thought had come from.

Brenda walked in without knocking and looked over his shoulder at the screen. 'Something I should know about?' she asked brightly. 'If it's something to do with our jewel smuggler, I don't think I want to know. And if it's something you're exploring just for the fun of it, I don't want to know that, either. Perhaps I should go back out and come in again later.'

Noel sighed. This is why he wanted a lock on his door. People just walked in and out whenever they felt like it without so much as a by-your-leave. It was rude, to say the least.

He shut the lid of his laptop. 'Witches and warlocks, they evidently go together, and Cassandra Moon recently found out her father is still alive. She thought he was dead.'

'And you think he's a warlock?' Brenda shook her head sadly. 'If I were you, sir, I'd stop visiting Abracadabra. It's not doing you any good.'

Noel looked up at his detective in surprise. 'You know what the house is called?'

'Everyone knows what the house is called. That's why nobody goes there. Not that we believe any of the stories, of course, but no point in going there if you don't need to.'

He remembered being given a packet of salt to carry on his first visit to the house. 'I think Dora encourages the stories to keep you lot away. It's a lovely house.' He opened the notebook lying on his desk. 'But now you're here you can do something for me. Find out what the nearest hospital is to Miami Beach and ask if someone called Chris something was admitted on August 23rd. Some sort of gastric trouble. Probably food poisoning, I should think.' He looked down at his notes. 'If he was taken ill at the airport, he would have been taken to hospital automatically to make sure he wasn't infectious or contagious. If he got better he would presumably have taken a later flight, so check last-minute bookings for flights back to England later that day or early the next day.'

'You don't have his last name?'

'No. But his first name is Chris, presumably Christopher, and he has an Essex accent. Can't be too many of those booked into a Miami hospital on that particular date.'

'This is the sapphire smuggler, then?' When Noel nodded, she said, 'It might be easier to grab a flight over there and check him out personally. It's easier talking to people face to face.'

Noel grinned at her. 'Nice try, Brenda, but I have no intention of sending you on an expenses-paid trip to Miami. I agree face to face is often a better way to interact with people, so you can use Skype if you want to. I'll allow that.'

'Thank you, sir.' Brenda gave him the finger behind her back as she went out of the door and Noel smiled. She was a good detective and she would get him exactly what he wanted, even if she didn't get her trip to Miami.

He flipped the pages of his notebook. He didn't have much more information on the smuggling case, even after meeting Rachel Saunders. She seemed genuine enough, but he needed to find the man who had given her the sapphires. What puzzled him was how the smuggler was going to get the necklace back. Approach Rachel out on the street, maybe? No, that would only work if she were wearing the necklace at the time. He needed an invitation in to her home, so he would get in touch with her one way or the other, of that Noel was certain. Someone out there was waiting for those stones to be delivered.

That thought gave him another idea and he called out for Kevin. Kevin was his youngest detective and liked nothing better than being in at the very start of a case. Noel couldn't help smiling as Kevin came through the door. He looked like an eager puppy waiting for his master to throw him a ball.

'Get on to the MPD and check

recent robberies of jewellery and precious stones in the area, particularly five top-grade sapphire gemstones that may have gone missing.' He looked up to find Kevin still standing in front of the desk. 'Is that a problem?'

'I guess it's the smuggling case,' Kevin said, looking uncomfortable. 'But I don't know what MPD is.'

'No reason why you should,' Noel said easily. 'It's the Miami Police Department.' As Noel watched Kevin leave his office he decided he must try not to embarrass the young man so often, but Kevin was easily embarrassed. He spent most of his spare time swotting up on everything he thought a detective should know, and hated to be caught out. On a number of occasions Noel had told him it would all come with experience, but Kevin wanted it all right now. Brenda had bought him a deerstalker hat and a magnifying glass on his last birthday.

Having given his two detectives something to do that would probably take them the rest of the day, Noel decided to get back on his computer and try to track down Cassandra's father. He wasn't looking for a warlock this time, he was hunting a real flesh-and-blood man — something he was quite good at. He had learnt a long time ago that everyone leaves a trail. Hector — aka Henry or Harry — Moon was out there somewhere, but the man could be literally anywhere in the world. And he could be using a different name. Noel sighed. Perhaps this was going to be more difficult than he had expected. He tried Googling several different variations of the name, but nothing came up. Moon was a more common surname than he had expected.

Dora had said her husband was good at doing a vanishing trick, but she didn't have Noel's resources. He had access to several archives that weren't available to the general public. Although there was nothing current, he discovered that Hector Moon (commonly known as Harry) had previously been a Royal Navy SEAL and had a commendation for bravery. Then approximately five years ago the man had moved to some obscure government office and disappeared. For the last five years there was no record of anyone called Hector Moon. Another change of name, maybe, or a complete change of identity? Noel had no way of knowing. He had always been of the opinion that no one could disappear completely, whether they were dead or alive, but there was always the exception that proved the rule.

He pursed his lips. Of course there was a much easier way of finding out the information he wanted — ask Dora. But she would want to know why he was checking up on her wayward husband, and he hadn't really got an answer, so that was something else he would have to put on the back burner for the time being. Families are strange things.

His own family roots had nothing to do with the smuggling case, but there was a chance his ancestry might have something to do with his strange ability to channel electricity when the need arose

— and his empathy with Cassandra Moon. The trouble was, without asking his grandmother a lot of questions, and possibly upsetting her, he had no way of finding out.

Find her, for together you will be invincible.

Noel frowned. Where had he heard those words before? And why had they popped into his head right now? Dora had once said something similar, but not those exact words. She had told him Cass would always be at his side. He could go along with that. He smiled to himself. They were bound together by something, either a strange form of static electricity, or fate, and he was quite happy to have the pretty redhead by his side if that was what it took to save the world.

He looked at his watch and realised he had wasted rather a lot of time on something that had nothing to do with police work. Maybe it was time to give up chasing phantoms and get back to solving crimes.

★ ★ ★

A woman arrived at the house late that evening with three cats in a basket. Cass got to the front door before her mother, but Dora was right on her heels. 'It will be someone with my cat, Cassie.'

Cass opened the door not knowing what to expect. A grizzled witch with a pointy hat wouldn't have surprised her, but the lady standing on the step was quite young and quite ordinary-looking. She was smartly dressed in a navy-blue skirt and lemon blouse, high-heeled shoes on her small feet, and a large wicker basket in each hand.

'My goodness, these animals are heavy. The stupid taxi driver refused to come up the lane and you've got potholes. I nearly broke my neck.'

Cass took the baskets, feeling her knees buckle as the animals moved inside. The woman gave Cass a grateful nod of thanks and they both followed Dora into the kitchen. Cass was glad to

100

put the heavy baskets on the floor, surprised the cats inside hadn't made a single sound of protest in spite of being bounced around in a taxi and then plonked down on the hard floor.

'There were only three animals ready,' the woman said, 'and one of them is a male. I was only going to bring the queens, but I was told you wanted to see them all. He's really heavy,' she added resentfully. 'He weighs as much as the other two put together, and he won't choose you. He'll want a man.'

Dora smiled. 'We'll see. Would you like something to drink? A cup of tea?'

The woman shook her head. 'No thanks. I have to get back to the other animals. We've got two sickly owls at the moment needing constant attention.' She smiled at Cass. 'I run an animal rescue centre, but I take in the special ones as well. One of the owls is a messenger, like in Harry Potter.'

'Oh, I see,' Cass said, although she didn't. She had no idea what the woman was talking about. 'Can we have a look at the cats?' She would have liked a kitten, but her mother obviously preferred to give a home to a rescue animal.

'Sure,' the woman said. 'I hope you get to keep one, I don't want to lug all three back up your drive. My name is Artemis, by the way, but most people call me Amy.'

'There is one taxi driver who will come up to the back gate,' Dora said. 'He'll risk it for a good tip. I'll give him a call when we've seen the cats.'

The baskets were moved to the middle of the rug on the kitchen floor and Amy lifted both the lids. Cass was surprised to see the basket lids hadn't been fastened down in any way. All three cats stepped out at the same moment and stood looking around. Cass had been expecting to see shiny black coats, and was surprised at the mix of colours. One of the two females was a dark tortoiseshell with bands of black and tan running through chocolate brown.

The other female was pale grey, almost white, with enormous blue eyes.

The male reminded Cass of a tiger. Big and heavy, with a thick coat of black stripes on gold, he had a broad face and small ears with tufts of pale fur at the tips. His eyes were gleaming amber, his feet enormous. His long tail moved slowly back and forth without any hint of animosity, and Cass thought he looked as if he were smiling.

Dora sat cross-legged on the floor and waited while all three animals examined her. The two females gave her a cursory inspection and then stepped daintily back into their basket. The big male took his time. He walked over to Dora and stared into her eyes, his tail quite still now. She held out a hand and he sniffed it, then he rubbed his face against hers and purred deep in his chest. She stood up and he sat by her side, still purring.

'Well I never,' Amy said. 'He chose you, a female. I've never seen that before. No wonder he's been difficult to place.'

Dora ran her hand down the cat's arched back. 'He's been waiting for me. I'm sorry I took so long,' she said to the cat.

The woman pulled a folded sheet of paper out of her pocket. 'You have to sign for him, and I need a name to put on the form.'

'His name is Tobias,' Dora said, taking the form. She signed it and added the cat's name, handing it back to Amy. 'Thank you for bringing him to me.'

'My pleasure,' Amy said. 'Can you call me that cab, please? I need to get back.'

Cass closed the door behind the woman called Artemis and walked back into the kitchen. The cat had claimed a chair near the stove and Cass looked at him thoughtfully. Even asleep he looked powerful, and judging by the scar running down her arm made by the little black cat, he was probably capable of inflicting more damage than a Rottweiler.

'Why Tobias?' she asked her mother.

Dora had been in the process of

filling the kettle, but she looked round in surprise. 'Because that's his name, of course. You can't shorten it, though. He won't be called Toby.'

'I'll try and remember that,' Cass said as she took two mugs from the cupboard. She'd hate to get on the wrong side of the animal asleep on the chair. She had marks to show what happens if you annoy a member of the cat family. 'Is he hungry, do you think?' She wondered what they would feed the beast. He looked as if a haunch of venison might be his usual dish of the day.

'He'll let us know if he wants something to eat.' Dora took the mug of tea Cass handed to her. 'He should be an asset. He's clever and strong. I'm glad he waited for me.'

Cass agreed with her mother. She had thought of asking if she could have the pale female, but she had a feeling Tobias might not like a housemate. He looked like a cat who walked by himself. She hoped he would prove to be a match for the black hellcat if it appeared again.

6

Rachel telephoned Cass a week later, just about the time Cass was thinking she couldn't really stall much longer. Chris had turned up on Rachel's doorstep and apologised profusely for leaving her at the airport. 'He told me he'd been really sick,' she said. 'He flew back as soon as he was allowed out of hospital. He was really nice, and I felt bad for thinking he had just dumped me.'

'Did you tell him about the necklace?' Cass asked.

'Yes, but I didn't tell him what you had done to it. I told him one of the flowers had broken and he thinks it just needed a bit of a repair. I'm dying to see his face when he sees how pretty those blue stones look set in gold.'

So am I, Cass thought. There was every chance it would be quite a shock for Mr Dempsey.

Rachel asked Cass how long it would be before the necklace was finished and ready to wear.

'Technically it's already finished and ready to pick up, but I still have to clean it up, and there are a couple of tests I'd like to do before I hand it over.'

'Can you bring it over sometime tomorrow afternoon then, please? Chris is coming round, and I can't wait for him to see it now it's finished.'

'Yes, of course I can. I'm sure I can finish my checks by then.' She had run out of excuses to hang on to the necklace. If she hedged any longer it would start to look suspicious.

She phoned Noel and he said he would be at the house in about twenty minutes. She left her studio, walked into the kitchen, and told her mother Noel was on his way. The cat looked up and then went back to sleep.

'What do we do now?' Cass asked Noel before he had time to shut the door. 'I've got to deliver the sapphires to Rachel tomorrow, and the smuggler guy will be at her house waiting for them.'

Noel closed the door and sat down at the kitchen table. 'You've finished resetting the stones, then?'

'Yes. I put the finishing touches to the necklace a couple of days ago.'

He breathed in and looked round the kitchen, suddenly noticing the cat. 'What in the name of all that's wonderful is that thing over there? It looks as if it belongs in a zoo.'

'That's Tobias, my cat,' Dora said proudly. 'He's quite impressive, isn't he?'

'You could say that.'

Cass remembered Noel's allergy. 'Are you OK?' she asked him worriedly. 'We can go into another room, if you like.' She didn't suggest moving Tobias because she wasn't sure that would be possible.

'I'm fine.' He walked across the room for a closer look. 'The black cat got me spooked for some reason, but I have no problem with this one.' He reached out a hand and the cat raised its head. Cass was just about to call out a warning, but Noel was already scratching Tobias under the chin and the cat seemed to like it.

'Wow,' she said. 'He won't let me do that. He's very much Dora's cat, and he doesn't much like anyone else touching him.'

Dora looked at Noel petting the cat, a smile hovering around her mouth. 'That's interesting.'

Noel sat back down at the kitchen table. 'We need a plan,' he said. 'Suppose you leave the necklace locked in your safe and invite Rachel and the smuggler to come here, to your studio, instead of you going to her place. That way you're on home territory. You can find a reason to make some adjustment to the necklace. Alter the length of the chain, maybe. I don't know. Then I can call in unannounced and you can act surprised. Rachel already thinks I'm your boyfriend, so it would be normal for me to drop in now and again, wouldn't it?'

Cass looked sceptical. 'That's a plan?

It sounds more like a spur-of-the-moment idea conjured up out of desperation.'

'Can you think of anything better?' He looked at Dora. 'All suggestions will be welcome.'

'That should work,' Dora said. 'The man can't cause much trouble with you there, can he? And if Cassie insists the necklace needs adjusting, he can't take it away with him.'

'How about knives and guns and snatching and running?' Cass said. 'That might work, too. How about Noel just arrests him?'

'What for?' Noel asked. 'All the man will have done is come to look at a necklace — which actually belongs to him, if you think about it. Even if we can prove the stones are quality sapphires, who's to say they aren't his? I'm still waiting for information about robberies in Miami. The trouble is, the rich and famous don't like to admit their billion-dollar mansion with all the latest technology can still be broken into. It makes them feel stupid.'

'So we let him come to my studio; I get the necklace out of the safe, complete with quality sapphires, let him handle it, and then tell him he can't have it. That's your plan?' Cass looked at Noel in disbelief. 'I sincerely hope Rachel is right and he really is a nice man, because he needs to be a very even-tempered nice man.'

'Oh, come on, Cassie,' Dora said. 'Where's your sense of adventure?'

'Why do I feel like a piece of cheese; the bait in the mousetrap?' She looked at Noel. 'What are you going to do if the nice man has a gun?'

He smiled at her. 'I'm sure I'll think of something.'

'Why does that not reassure me?'

Dora was beginning to look quite interested, and that was a bad sign. Cass tried to keep any major confrontations well away from her. Maybe she could ask Tobias to sit in on the meeting, but at the moment he was asleep on his back and looked more like a teddy bear than a tiger.

'See if you can organise a viewing for tomorrow afternoon,' Noel said. 'I've got some work to do in the morning, but the sooner we do this, the better. Then if you can stall him for a few more days it will give me time to chase up the Miami side of things. For all we know, this guy may go backwards and forwards with pieces of stolen jewellery all the time. At the moment I have no idea whether this is a big operation or just a small-time, fly-by-night thing.' He looked at Cass. 'Did you say Rachel actually wore the necklace through customs? I'm surprised no one asked her where she got it.'

'The setting was obviously cheap, and the stones had been painted with something to dull them down a bit — I don't know what, but it came off quite easily when I cleaned them.'

'You still knew they were real, though, the moment you saw them.'

'It's my job to know gemstones. Even if a customs officer thought the stones might be real sapphires, they could have legitimately belonged to Rachel. I'm sure some people wear expensive jewellery when they fly. He wouldn't link it to a robbery even if he had a picture of the sapphires. The necklace would have looked completely different.' She tried to imagine what the beautiful blue stones had looked like in all their original glory, and wondered if she would ever know.

★ ★ ★

Cass looked at her watch again. They should be here any minute, and she was feeling decidedly nervous. As far as she knew, Chris Dempsey was a criminal, possibly a violent one, and he might walk in and start waving a gun around. She paced the studio, wishing Noel would arrive early so she had some support. If it came to a showdown, she would hand the stones over without a word of protest. It would be his fault if they disappeared forever.

The sound of car tyres on gravel had

her moving towards the door. The heavy oak gave nothing away and she wished she had a spy hole so she could see who was outside. She had taken the necklace out of the safe on the assumption that Dempsey might be able to memorise the safe code if she opened it in front of him. She couldn't exactly shield the keypad with her hand as if she were putting in her pin number at Tesco. That might look a tad suspicious.

When someone knocked, she opened the door and stood back, not knowing quite what to expect. She hadn't thought to ask Rachel what Chris looked like. She had guessed he must be reasonably good-looking, but the man standing in front of her was still quite a shock. Although he wasn't her type, she could see why Rachel had been bowled over. Christopher Dempsey was probably a fraction under six feet tall, blond, and tanned a *Baywatch* gold. His pecs, visible through his thin white T-shirt, told of long hours in the gym. She was quite sure he had a six-pack other men would be willing to die for.

He placed his hand gently on Rachel's back and let her precede him through the doorway. Obviously a gentleman as well, Cass thought; not the sort of man you would expect to smuggle sapphires across the Atlantic. But she had learnt a long time ago not to trust her eyes. Her mother didn't look much like a witch, after all.

At that pont Noel arrived and introduced himself to Dempsey, saying he was a friend and had only popped in to ask Cass out for dinner that evening. He didn't actually say the word 'boyfriend', but he didn't have to. From the tone of his voice and his possessive glance her way, anyone would have made exactly the assumption he wanted them to.

Cass watched Dempsey as his eyes roved around her studio. He was either taking a genuine interest in her workplace, or he was casing the joint. As far as she was aware she had never met a smuggler before, so it was difficult to tell.

Dempsey had moved to her display cabinet. 'You do beautiful work, Miss Moon. I'm afraid the necklace I bought Rachel isn't up to this sort of standard.'

'No problem,' Cass said, watching him closely. 'Even though the necklace has broken, the blue stones are really lovely.' She still couldn't make up her mind about him, but she thought she could see a bead of sweat on his upper lip.

'It's really nice to meet you both,' Noel said, 'but I don't want to get in the way. I should be going.'

Cass jumped in quickly. What was the matter with the man? She wasn't going to let him walk out and leave her with a potentially dangerous criminal. 'You don't need to go, Noel. You saw the original drawings, so you must stay and see the changes I've made.' She was looking at Noel, but out of the corner of her eye she saw the look of shock on Dempsey's face. He hadn't been expecting any changes. He must have thought it was just a repair job.

116

'If you're sure I won't be in the way, I'd love to see the necklace.' Noel smiled at Rachel. 'A beautiful girl like you deserves something special.'

Cass frowned. Now what was he up to? Chatting up Rachel wasn't going to endear him to Dempsey, but perhaps that was the idea. Get the man riled up enough and he might slip up. Alternatively, he might wait until he had the necklace safely in his hot little hand and then kill them all.

Cass picked up the velvet bag lying on her workbench. 'Your necklace has cleaned up beautifully, Rachel. I hope you like the new setting.' This time Dempsey's reaction almost made her laugh. He wasn't a very good actor.

'New setting?' he said, his voice going up a notch. 'Rachel didn't tell me anything about a new setting.'

Rachel was almost dancing with excitement. 'Because it was a secret, silly. I loved the necklace you gave me, but one of the little flowers had broken and it couldn't be repaired.' She kissed him quickly on the cheek. 'I've kept the pretty stones. You'll love what Cass has done with them, I know you will.'

Cass slid the necklace out of the velvet bag, her eyes still on Dempsey, and spread it out on her workbench. Now the necklace only had three flowers instead of the original five. The petals were made of gold wire, each one delicately crafted to show off the deep blue sapphire nestling in the centre. The remaining two stones had been made into matching drop earrings.

If Cass hadn't been sure of Dempsey's guilt before, his expression right at that moment left no doubt in her mind whatsoever. The poor man looked positively sick.

Rachel gave a squeal of delight. 'It's beautiful! The earrings as well. I just love it all.' In her delight she kissed Chris full on the lips. 'See? I told you it would be beautiful.' She turned to Cass. 'Thank you so much! Can I try them on?'

'Of course you can.'

Chris was a big, strong man, but right

now he looked as if he wanted to cry. Cass saw him watching her as she looped the glittering necklace round Rachel's slim neck. He pulled himself together fairly quickly and moved towards Rachel for a closer look at the stones.

'You're right, Rachel,' he said. 'It's lovely. You do clever work, Miss Moon. The necklace definitely looks very different from when I gave it to Rachel. You'd think those blue beads were worth a fortune, wouldn't you? You've make them look like the real thing.'

'All I did was clean them up,' Cass said. 'The stones may be some form of synthetic, or even glass. Paste stones were used in a lot of early jewellery and looked exactly like the real thing.' She turned to Rachel. 'Paste is a form of glass with a high lead content to give it extra brilliance, and it can look fantastic. The earlier stones were cut the same way as gemstones, and even expert jewellers had trouble telling the difference.'

She looked at Dempsey. He was obviously guilty, but just how guilty she still wasn't sure. 'I think your little blue stones had already been reset once before. I don't know where you got the necklace, but I don't think it was in the original setting when you bought it.' She gave him one of her best smiles. 'And please, call me Cass. Everyone else does.'

'I got the necklace in some little shop near Miami Beach. It wasn't very expensive, and the stones looked pretty.' He tried a smile as well, but it wavered a little. 'It made me think of Rachel, so I bought it for her.' When she smiled at him he put an arm round her shoulders. 'We must be going, Rachel. We don't want to outstay our welcome, do we?'

Cass saw Noel shoot her a look. She knew he didn't want Rachel walking out with the necklace, but he wasn't being much help. 'The clasp felt a little loose when I did it up,' she told Rachel. 'Can I have another look at it before you go? I don't want you to lose the necklace on your way home.' She walked round behind Rachel, undid the necklace and laid it on her workbench again. 'The safety catch isn't holding properly. It's got a tiny button that should stop it coming undone accidentally, but for some reason the catch doesn't seem to be working.'

Rachel leant over the bench. 'Can you fix it?'

Cassandra fiddled with the safety catch for a few moments and then shook her head. 'I'm really sorry, but it's going to need a new clasp and I haven't got one here at the moment. Don't worry, I can get one in a couple of days and fix it for you.'

'A couple of days?' Dempsey stared at her in obvious panic. 'Rachel wants the necklace now, don't you, sweetheart? We came over here specially to pick it up.' He looked at Cass suspiciously. 'Are you quite sure there's something wrong with it?'

Cass handed the necklace to him. She wasn't stupid enough to pretend there was something wrong if there

121

wasn't. She watched him play with the clasp and then took it back from him. 'See? That little button should stay in when you push it. It's supposed to stop the necklace coming undone accidentally, but it's not working.'

'I would have thought you'd have the tools to fix it right here in your studio.'

'Sorry, but I buy the safety clasps from a supplier. Now I know the problem, I'll make sure the new one is working properly. And once I get the new clasp, it will only take a few moments to put it on the necklace.'

'I think we should take it with us, Rachel. You won't lose it if you only wear it indoors. You can bring it back here when Miss Moon has the new clasp.'

'It will be fine, Chris,' Rachel said gently. 'I can wait a few more days, and I really need to make sure the necklace can't fall off, even round the house.' She sighed. 'It's so pretty now, isn't it? And the blue stones look far nicer set in gold.'

'How about I pour us all a drink?' Noel said. He clapped Chris on the shoulder, making him wince, and then buddy-punched him on the arm. 'It seems Rachel really likes the necklace, even if she can't take it home today. You should be pleased. She did all this for you, you know.'

Chris looked as if he wanted to punch Noel back, a lot harder and not on the arm, but he managed a smile. 'Sure, a drink would be great. Just a small one, though. I'm driving.'

Cass had been watching Dempsey carefully. She had seen the look of panic in his eyes when he first saw the necklace, but she was pretty sure this wasn't Chris Dempsey's scam. There was someone else pulling the strings. Someone a lot higher up in the chain of command. Someone who could make Dempsey look as if he were about to pass out or throw up and wasn't quite sure which to do first.

Noel was thoroughly enjoying himself. Cass could see the look of satisfaction on his face as he handed Rachel her glass of wine. Making sure Dempsey was watching, he let his fingers trail over the girl's wrist. She took the glass of Prosecco and gave him a coquettish smile. Cass tried to catch Noel's eye. Sometimes he could go too far.

She still hadn't quite made up her mind about Christopher Dempsey. With his sun-bleached hair and Miami tan, he could have stepped straight out of a surfer movie, but she had seen the way he looked at Rachel. Maybe he really did care for her. Not that it would matter if Rachel was the love of his life, because if Noel had his way Chris would still finish up in jail. Right now he was looking as jumpy as a frog on a hot brick, and Cass was afraid Noel might have gone that one step too far.

There was a soft knock on the inside door, and when Cass opened it Dora poked her head tentatively into the room. 'I wondered if anyone would like a cup of tea. I've just made a pot.'

Cass rolled her eyes. She should have known her mother wouldn't be able to resist a peek at Rachel and her boy-friend, but it was Dempsey who spoke first.

'Thank you,' he said politely, putting his empty glass on the workbench. 'But we have to be going, don't we, Rachel?'

Rachel looked as if that were the last thing she wanted to do. With Noel being overly attentive just to annoy Chris, and Chris doing his best to compete with Noel, she was enjoying all the attention.

She pouted prettily, but let him take her arm. 'You must be Cass's mum. Thank you, Mrs Moon, but we've already stayed too long.' She turned to Cass. 'Let me know when the necklace is finished and I'll come and pick it up. I think it is absolutely beautiful, so thank you again.'

Cass smiled. 'You're paying for it, Rachel, so you deserve a perfect neck-lace. I'm sorry about the faulty clasp. A couple of days at the most and it'll be ready.'

As Rachel reached the door, she turned back towards them. 'Oh, by the way, your cat was waiting at the gate so we let it into the garden.'

The silence was so intense it positively hummed. Rachel frowned. 'I'm sorry, I thought it was your cat. Shouldn't we have let it in?'

Dora moved further into the room. 'It shouldn't have been able to come in,' she muttered to herself. 'What colour was the cat?'

'Black, I think.' Looking slightly confused, Rachel turned to Chris. 'It *was* black, wasn't it? A pretty little thing. It rubbed round my legs and meowed until we opened the gate for it.'

Cass gave her mother a warning look. 'Oh, we know that one. It's not ours; it belongs to a neighbour.'

Dora frowned. 'Did you speak to it? Did you invite it in?'

Rachel was beginning to look thoroughly spooked and Cass knew she was going to have to come up with an explanation for Dora's behaviour. 'The black cat is normally quite nervous and doesn't come any further than our gate,' she said. 'My mother thought you must have spoken to it to get it come inside.'

'Oh, I see,' Rachel said, obviously relieved to find she wasn't in the same room as a mad woman. 'I think I said something like, 'Come on in then, I can't hold the gate open forever.' Something like that. Do you want us to go and look for it? It must still be in the garden because I shut the gate once it was inside.'

Noel opened the outside door. 'I'll walk you to the front gate. That little cat may appear all sweetness and light, but it can be quite vicious if it feels like it.'

'If you see it, don't try to pick it up,' Dora said. 'It scratched Cass the other day.'

Rachel paused in the doorway again. 'I'm so sorry. After all you've done for me, I've gone and let a nasty, spiteful little cat into your garden. It did seem quite gentle at the time. Perhaps if you leave the gate open, it will go out again.'

Chris tugged at Rachel's arm. 'Let's go, Rachel. If we see the cat we'll shoo it away.'

7

'I wish it were that simple,' Dora said as Cass closed the door. 'Tobias knew something was wrong. He's been fussing for the last hour. That's why I came to see you.' She glanced down as Tobias appeared at her side. 'He went out through the cat flap earlier but came back in a few moments later. I think he was waiting for your visitors to leave.'

'Or he's as scared of the black hellcat as we are.'

Noel came back inside. 'No sign of it. Not out in the open, anyway. I didn't shake the bushes.'

'Coward,' Cass said.

'Tobias will find it when he's ready.' Dora held open the door into the house. 'Let's go back to the kitchen and you can tell me all about Rachel and her friend.'

'That Christopher Dempsey is as guilty as hell,' Noel said once they were seated round the kitchen table. 'I saw his face when you tipped the necklace out of the bag. Sheer disbelief. He couldn't believe what he was seeing.'

'I don't understand why it mattered what it looked like. He only wanted the stones.'

'I think he was going to swap it for one that looked the same. That would have been a good scheme, and really quite easy if everything had gone according to plan. He lets Rachel wear the stones through customs and then waits for an opportunity to make the switch. She wouldn't have had the necklace long enough to notice any slight differences.'

Cass nodded. 'But everything started to go wrong when he got taken ill at the airport.'

'And now I expect someone is breathing down his neck waiting to get their sapphires back.'

Dora put two mugs of fresh tea on

the table. 'So what do you think he's going to do now?'

'I don't know,' Noel said grimly. 'That's why I'm worried. I want to take the necklace back to Norton police station and put it in our lockup box. Dempsey might try to break into the safe in the studio, and I don't want either of you in any more danger than necessary.'

'No.' Cass shook her head. She was fed up with him telling her what to do. 'No. The necklace stays here. Besides, I don't think Chris is dangerous, and why would he try to get it out of a safe when he thinks I'm going to give it back to Rachel in a few days? He'll wait until she puts it down somewhere in her flat and just take it.'

'He wouldn't be able to get into your studio, anyway,' Dora said. 'Nothing human can get past the protection I've set up.'

Nothing human? Cass wondered what Dora thought was out there. She knew her mother had a good imagination, but worrying about a petty thief breaking into the house was quite enough. She didn't want to think about spooky things that go bump in the night. Someone had to keep a hold on reality.

Tobias wandered across the kitchen and disappeared from sight. Dora watched him as he walked through into the tiny scullery where the washing machine and tumble dryer were kept. 'He's got a cat flap in there,' she told Noel. 'He keeps going outside to look around and then comes back in again. I think he knows exactly where the black cat is. He's waiting until it gets dark.'

'Will she hurt him?' Cass asked worriedly, rubbing her arm. She had become used to having the big golden cat around, and she still had the scars from her own encounter with the hellcat.

Dora gave a small sigh. 'I don't think so. I hope not.'

'You realise you're both talking as if the black cat is female,' Noel said.

'Because it is. Or as near female as a

132

thing like that can be. Tobias is waiting until it gets dark. There's a full moon tonight so her powers will be at their strongest. But so will his.'

'Can't we keep him in?' Cass asked. 'I don't want that vicious thing to hurt him.'

Dora smiled. 'He's got under your skin, hasn't he? I thought you didn't like cats.'

'I never said that,' Cass said defensively. But Dora was right; Tobias had captured a little piece of her heart. Sometimes when she couldn't sleep she would go down to the kitchen for a warm drink, and he was always there, ready to rub his blunt head against her legs and sit with her until she was ready to go back to bed. Sometimes he went upstairs with her and curled up at her feet. She would never admit to it, because he was only a cat, but he made her feel safe.

Noel offered to stay the night. If there was going to be a skirmish with the hellcat, he thought he should be there, but Dora shook her head. 'We'll keep you in reserve,' she said. 'A secret weapon.'

He gave Cass a puzzled look and she grinned at him. 'I shall think of you like that from now on. A secret weapon of mass destruction.'

'Take care, both of you,' he said as he left, and Cass wished she had asked him to stay.

★ ★ ★

Something disturbed her in the night. Maybe a sound — perhaps a sudden draft — or just a tingle in her fingertips. She wasn't quite sure what had caused her to sit up in bed, her heart beating twice as fast as normal. But now she was wide awake, still and silent, her ears pricked to detect any unusual sound. Noel had seriously upset a man they believed to be a criminal, and she hadn't exactly helped when she told him he couldn't have his sapphires back. Was he in her studio right now trying to open her safe?

Cass swung her feet out of bed and pulled on her dressing gown, a short wraparound in dark blue velvet. It gave her more confidence than wandering around in her birthday suit. She debated between bare feet or slippers, and stuck with bare feet. Easier to run if she had to. She paused again before she opened her bedroom door. Switching on every light would be sensible, but she didn't want to wake her mother if there was no need, and she hadn't heard another sound since she sat up in bed.

Tobias, she told herself, as she made her way along the dark landing. It must have been the cat prowling around. He was usually quiet at night, but then tonight wasn't exactly like any other night. The hellcat was loose in the garden.

She tiptoed down the stairs, trying not to make any noise in case someone was lurking in the hallway below. She still hadn't heard any more strange sounds, so maybe it was her imagination playing tricks. She stood quite still on the bottom stair. There it was again. The sound wasn't coming from her studio; it was coming from the kitchen. The door from the kitchen to the hallway was slightly open, and a shaft of pale light crossed the floor in front of her. Still on tiptoe, Cass eased the door open a few more inches and peered inside. She caught her breath when she saw the French doors to the patio were wide open. Moonlight was streaming into the kitchen, and just outside the open doors a figure stood out in stark silhouette. Cass was about to grab a cast-iron pan from the stove and crack the intruder over the head, when the figure turned round and Cass realised it was her mother.

'Why have you got the doors open? You know the hellcat is out there.'

Dora put a finger to her lips and then beckoned Cass over. 'I know,' she whispered. 'I can see it sitting in a tree with Tobias standing guard below.

Don't make too much noise or you'll break his concentration.'

Cass crept over to stand beside her mother. The slabs beneath her bare feet were cold, but the sight in front of her kept her rooted to the spot. The moon was low on the horizon and looked huge, a great silver orb perfectly framing an old, leafless tree. The black cat was sitting on one of the branches. She couldn't see Tobias, but if her mother said he was waiting down below, he probably was.

'Why is he keeping guard? Shouldn't he be seeing the hellcat off the premises?'

Dora looked at Cass as if she was being particularly stupid. 'Would you start a fight with that thing up in the branches of a tree? She's lighter than him, and faster. She'd make mincemeat of him up there. He knows she's got to come down some time, and he knows he can beat her on the ground.'

'Are you sure, Mother?'

Dora sighed. 'No, I'm not sure. She's

faster, but he'll have all that weight behind him. He ought to be able to slaughter her — if she plays fair. But she won't, of course, and I don't know how much power she has.'

Although Cass despised herself for asking, she said, 'How about his power?'

Dora shook her head. 'I don't know that either, Cassie. I just don't know. Until I see him fight I have nothing to judge him by.' She looked down at Cass's feet. 'Come inside. This could take all night and you'll get cold. I'll make us a cup of tea.'

The solution to everything, Cass thought, as she followed her mother back into the kitchen. Dora shut the doors but left the blinds open. She didn't turn on the light because she didn't need to. A full moon, Cass thought. A good night for a cat fight.

Dora laced the tea with something: a clear liquid in a thin-necked bottle she took from a cupboard. Cass didn't ask what it was. She took a sip and felt the warmth seeping through to every part of her body. After that, she didn't much care what it was. She felt wide awake and ready to take on the hellcat herself.

'Can't we help him? What if I knock it out of the tree with a broom? You said Tobias can beat it on the ground.'

'I hope he can. Drink your tea, Cassie, and let Tobias handle this. He knows what he's doing.'

Cass had a suspicion her mother might be crossing her fingers behind her back, but she couldn't think of anything else to suggest. 'If he does get rid of it, will it be able to come back in again?'

'Not without an invitation. Why don't you go to bed, Cassie? There is nothing either of us can do to help him.'

'You're going to stay up, aren't you? And I can't go to bed knowing he's out there with that thing. I'll stay here with you.'

They sat for another hour before anything happened. Cass refused more tea because she was afraid she might miss something if she had to make a trip to the loo. The house had grown cold, so Dora warmed the kitchen up by turning on the oven. She said a spell could muddle the ether, whatever that meant. Even though they were waiting for something to happen, neither of them was prepared for the scream that echoed round the garden and reverberated off the walls of the house.

A sound like that couldn't possibly have come from a cat, Cass thought, as she leapt to her feet and rushed to the glass doors. She could see the hellcat clearly, still on the same branch. It was standing up now, its tail straight up in the air, looking down at something. Dora put a hand on her arm, making her jump.

'Don't open the door, Cassie. If she comes down she might be able to get inside the house. The moon is on her side tonight.' Dora suddenly gripped Cass's arm. 'Look! Tobias is halfway up the tree. He's going up after her.'

'Is that a good idea? You said she had

the advantage if she stayed in the tree.'

'He obviously thinks differently. Did you hear her scream? She must be worried. That's a good sign.'

Cass couldn't speak. She was watching Tobias as he made his way slowly up the trunk of the tree. The hellcat was still watching him, her back arched. Even at this distance Cass was sure she could see the black fur bristling in anger. If Tobias kept climbing he would soon be within reach of those lethal claws. She rubbed her arm in sympathy. She knew only too well how much damage those claws could do.

But the hellcat didn't wait. Rather than attack, she began to climb as well. Within a couple of minutes she was almost at the top of the tree. Here the branches were thinner and bent under her weight. Delicately, putting one paw in front of the other with extreme care, she moved to the end of a skinny, swaying branch and waited to see what the big cat would do.

Cass turned to look at her mother.

141

'He can't get to her there, can he? He's too heavy.'

'Clever,' Dora said, 'but what has it gained her?'

They soon found out. With a sudden burst of speed, the hellcat ran to the end of the skinny branch and launched herself into space, reaching with out-stretched claws for the branches of another nearby tree. Cass could see she was going to make it, and once she was safely in a different tree she could get down to the ground and away. But Tobias had moved as well, and just as fast. He was on a lower branch, but he took off with as much speed and agility as the hellcat — and caught her in mid-flight. Locked together, the two animals plummeted to the ground. Cass heard the thud as they landed, but she couldn't see either of them in the thick undergrowth.

Her mother stopped her opening the door into the garden. 'Leave them, Cassie,' Dora told her sharply. 'If you try and interfere they'll both hurt you.

Once an animal is in fight mode it will turn on anything that gets in its way.'

Cass closed her eyes. She knew her mother was right. She could hear both animals now through the closed doors. Tobias was growling the way only a tomcat can growl, and the hellcat was keening: a high-pitched wail that sent a shiver through Cass's body.

'Will she hurt him? I know you said he's heavier than she is, but she's so quick.' Cass could feel a tear running down her face and when her mother put an arm round her, she didn't protest. 'I don't want him to get hurt.' She wiped a hand across her face. 'He's not really that tough. Sometimes he comes and sleeps with me on my bed.'

'He's watching over you, Cassie. That's why I got him. He'll always try to keep us safe.'

Cass moved away from her mother and pressed her forehead against the window. The sounds had stopped and now the moonlit garden was eerily silent. There was nothing in the trees that she could see, but she had no idea where the two animals had gone after they fell to the ground. 'I can't see them,' she whispered. 'I can't see either of them.' She turned to face her mother. 'Do you think they're both dead?'

'Oh, for goodness sake, Cassie,' her mother said crossly. 'I very much doubt either of them is dead. Injured, probably, but we still can't go out there. We have to wait for Tobias to make his own way home.'

Cass wondered if it was the stuff Dora had put in her tea. She wasn't usually this emotional, particularly about an animal, but she felt near to tears again. 'What if he can't?'

'Then we'll have to wait for daylight.'

They both looked towards the scullery when the cat flap made its usual clunk. Cass stared at the door, but there was no sign of Tobias. Dora's hand was back on her daughter's arm.

'Wait, Cassie. She can't come into the house, but she'll do her best to make us go out there. That's her territory.'

'Maybe not anymore,' Cass said, as Tobias came slowly into the room. He was on his feet, but his paws were leaving bloody footprints on the stone floor with every step. His ear had been ripped and was hanging in shreds, and his nose looked a bit of a mess, but most of the blood was coming from a deep gash in his side. Cass blinked back yet more tears and sincerely hoped the hellcat looked a lot, lot worse.

Dora was already taking bottles out of her potion cupboard. 'Put a towel on the table, Cassie. I think we may have to lift him up. And do stop snivelling. As you can see, he's not dead yet, and we've got work to do.'

It took a while, but Tobias was quiet and patient, even when Dora got out a needle and thread and stitched the wound in his side. He purred through most of it, but Cass knew cats sometimes purr when they're in pain. She helped her mother as much as she could, but she knew if anyone could make Tobias better, it was Pandora Moon. Eventually the cat was cleaned, stitched and bandaged, and back on his chair by the stove.

'Is she still out there?' Cass asked.

Dora shook her head. 'No, I can't feel her around anymore, but I don't think she's dead. I think she left while she could, before he really did kill her. She won't bother us again for a while.'

'What did she want? Why was she so anxious to come into the house?'

Dora was washing her hands in the sink and didn't answer straight away. 'I'm not sure, Cassie. And even if I did know, I couldn't tell you. It's not my job.'

'Then whose job is it?' Cass said impatiently. She was fed up with all the secrecy. Tired of being scared for her mother's safety, and her own, and now Tobias's as well. Knowing the hellcat was still alive didn't help either. The nasty little creature deserved to die for what she had just done to Tobias.

Dora turned round from the sink, wiping her hands on a cloth. 'I have something to tell you.'

Cass felt her stomach knot. She didn't need any more surprises; she'd had enough for one night.

'Your father wants to see you,' Dora said. 'He's coming here, to the house.'

For a moment Cass couldn't speak. What her mother was saying couldn't possibly be true. Somewhere in the world there was a person who claimed to be her father, but she didn't know him. He was a person she had no memories of anywhere in her head. He might have suddenly decided he wanted to see her — but she didn't want to see him.

'When is he coming? Why does he want to see me now? He's never bothered before.'

'Because he thinks it's time, I suppose. I don't know how the man's mind works. I never have.'

'But it's been years and years. I don't even remember him from when I was a baby.'

'You don't remember him because he didn't want you to remember him, but he was living with us until you were about five. Your gifts have been hidden until now because you've kept them supressed. You still don't really believe, do you, Cassie?'

'Why now?' Cass asked again. The thought of seeing her father terrified her. What if he really was a warlock? She had seen pictures of wizards and warlocks — old men with beards and a pointy hat. Was that what her father looked like? Why had she never seen a picture of him? Cass asked her mother if she had one.

Dora was quiet for so long Cass thought she wasn't going to answer. 'Yes. But he'd kill me if he knew, and it was taken a few years ago so he probably looks different now. I cut it out of a newspaper.'

'Show me.'

Her mother could hardly refuse. This man who was supposedly her father had been thrust upon her out of the blue a few months ago. Her mother had never talked about him and she had assumed he was dead, possibly because she had no memories of him. She ought to be able to remember a man who had been in her life until she was five. Had he deliberately erased her memories? She shook her head in disbelief. Now she was getting as fanciful as her mother.

Dora opened a cupboard and reached inside. A flat folder had been hidden behind her potion bottles. She took the folder to the table and Cass followed, already wishing she had kept quiet. She didn't need to know what the man looked like. She intended to be well away from the house when he turned up.

Dora opened the flap and tipped the contents of the folder out onto the table. There was more than one photo and more than one newspaper cutting. Cass sat down on a chair next to her mother and realised a lot of the pictures were of a small child: a little girl with red-gold hair and a shy smile. Cass didn't remember anything about that child, but she

149

realised the photos must be of her. Most of them were with her mother but in one of them a tall, good-looking man with thick, dark hair held the little girl on his shoulders. They were both laughing.

'He didn't know I was taking this one,' Dora said with a smile. 'He never let me take photos of him.' She shuffled the newspaper cuttings until she came to one with a picture of a man in Royal Navy uniform. This man was older and he had a short, dark beard. A peaked cap with gold braiding covered his hair, but Cass could tell it was the same person.

'Why don't I remember him?'

Dora looked uncomfortable. 'You were very small when he went away. You hadn't even started school.'

And in a few days' time she would be twenty-nine. She felt cheated. She had been deprived of a parent for all those years. Not only a parent, but all memories of him as well. She remembered her school days perfectly, but nothing before that. She couldn't understand why it had never bothered her; why she had never asked any questions. Maybe her father had the answers.

8

The next day Noel was busy looking for answers as well. He had some information from the MPD about thefts in the Miami Beach area. There had been three fairly recent robberies where jewellery had been taken, but only one report mentioned sapphires. Noel flicked through the pages on his computer screen. Four perfectly matched blue sapphires and one slightly larger one. Origin, Burma. There was a picture of a heavy gold pendant set with three of the stones, including the largest one, and a pair of stud earrings set with two of the smaller ones.

He looked at his watch. He needed to talk to the man who owned the sapphires, but he was probably still in bed. He didn't want to antagonise the man, because he wanted information, and he needed to speak to Cass to find out if there was anything to distinguish the stones. From what he could gather the rightful owner of the stones should have a record of their weight. All he had to do was get Cass to weigh the ones she had in her safe and see if the weights matched.

He picked up the phone and waited for Cass to answer, but it was Dora's voice he heard. She never answered the phone if Cass was around.

'Where's Cass, Dora? Was there trouble with the black cat? Is Cass injured?' He was cursing himself for not phoning earlier. He shouldn't have left the two women alone in the house with that thing stalking the grounds.

'No, we're both fine, Noel. Tobias was hurt, but I patched him up, and the black cat has gone. We were all up most of the night, so I let Cass sleep in this morning.'

'Is it OK if I come round later? I need to speak to Cass about the sapphires. Can she weigh them, do you think?'

'I'm sure she can. Come round to lunch, Noel. Cassie is angry and upset, and she needs to talk to someone.'

He put down the phone wondering what Cass was upset about. If the black cat was gone, she should be feeling relieved. He worked until midday and then decided to try calling the American businessman before he left.

A woman answered, her American accent hardly noticeable. 'Chantelle speaking.'

'Mrs Blakely? Would it be possible to speak with your husband?'

'Gabe? I'm sorry, he's at work. Can I help you?'

Noel explained he was calling about the robbery and the woman was quite impressed when he said he might have found her sapphires.

'You found my jewellery in England? How extraordinary.'

'We have to check it out first. Does your husband have a description of the jewellery and the cut and weight of the sapphires?'

'I'm sure he does. He's handling the insurance claim. Someone burglarised us while we were out. I changed my mind about wearing the blue stones at the last minute because they didn't go with my dress. He's blaming me because I left them out on the bedside table.'

'We recovered five stones, Mrs Blakely. Four small ones and a bigger one.'

'That is correct. The sapphires were set in a three-stone necklace, with the big stone in the middle, and the remaining two were made into a pair of stud earrings. All of them were set in gold. My husband has already put in a claim with the insurance company, but now he'll have to let them know the jewellery has been recovered.'

She was making it sound as if the recovery of the stones was more of a nuisance than the robbery.

'I am afraid the stones were removed from their original setting,' Noel told her. 'So an accurate description of the sapphires is a necessary precaution. I will need to ask your husband to fax me a copy of the description he gave your insurers. Perhaps I could telephone again when he's at home.'

'He works very strange hours, Detective. Men in my husband's position always do.'

Noel put the phone back on his desk. Millionaires weren't the only ones who worked strange hours, he thought. The Mr Plods of this world did it as well. With a little smile he picked up his jacket and set off for lunch at the house called Abracadabra.

On the drive to the house, he thought how strange it was that Cass had chosen exactly the same arrangement of stones for the setting she had designed: three in the necklace and a pair of earrings. Perhaps Dora was right when she said gemstones talked to Cass.

Dora had cold roast chicken and salad set out on the kitchen table, Cass was filling a pitcher with something pink, and the doors to the patio were open. He hadn't realised until then what a beautiful day it was. The last of summer going out in style. Dora's roses had produced a second flush of pink flowers and the scent filled the kitchen.

'Pimms,' Cass said. 'Or our interpretation of it.'

'Pleasantly intoxicating,' Dora said, 'but it won't show up on a breathalyser. I'm glad you could come, Noel. Sit down and relax.'

He sat as instructed, but he wasn't relaxed. Not yet, anyway. Perhaps a few glasses of the pink stuff would help. Cass looked as wound up as the proverbial spring, and he wondered what her problem was. The big tiger-cat was sprawled on a chair asleep, but Noel had seen one eye inch open when he came into the kitchen. The cat had a bandage on his leg and a row of black stiches down his side. His left ear looked pretty mangled as well, but none of it seemed to be bothering him.

Noel waited until Cass had filled his glass and then he took a sip. Sweet fruit with a zing of something he couldn't quite place. He wondered if Dora had a still somewhere. Most alcohol comes from natural ingredients, and he knew Dora prided herself on using the most natural ingredients around.

'What happened last night?' he asked.

Cass slid onto a chair next to him and picked up her own glass. 'Tobias was a hero. He took off from halfway up a tree and caught the hellcat in mid-air. She wasn't expecting him to do that. She thought she was safe up in the skinny little branches, because he's so heavy, but he was cleverer than she was. He wanted to get her on the ground where he could use the advantage of his weight. We heard them fighting for a while before he came in.' She paused for a moment, remembering. 'Anyway, Mother patched him up and the hellcat is gone, so we're both really proud of him.'

'Good. I'm glad Tobias wasn't hurt too much. I felt bad about leaving you here on your own. I should have stayed.'

Cass helped herself to chicken and passed the dish to Noel. 'We're fine. Dora said you wanted to ask me something.'

'I came round to ask you about the sapphires. We think we've found the owner — a Mr Blakely who lives in Miami. Did you weigh the stones before you reset them?'

'Yes. The four smaller ones are all the same weight. The big one is different, of course. I have it all written down in my studio. I'll find it for you when we've finished lunch.'

He glanced at Dora and she gave him a brief nod. Being alone in the studio with Cass would not be a problem, but she had a habit of slamming the studio door in his face. She liked her own space and hated anyone invading her privacy. He knew he had asked a lot of her in the last few days. The other thing she hated was lying, and he had made her do that as well. All he could do now was try and make it up to her any way he could.

Cass was exceptionally quiet, but Dora kept the conversation going through the meal. She told him all about the cat fight and what a hero Tobias had been. She made it sound as if a fight between a cat from hell and a witch's familiar was the most normal thing in the world. He helped clear the table and then followed Cass to her studio, almost bumping into her when she stopped outside the door.

'I won't be a minute, Noel. You can wait here.'

'No, I'm not going to wait outside. I need to tell you something, Cass. I telephoned the woman in America who owned the necklace.' When she reluctantly opened the door he followed her inside. 'Mr Blakely has already made a claim with his insurance company, so it gets a bit complicated. The stones are no longer in the original setting.'

'Does it matter?' Cass asked with a shrug. 'If it happened in America, it's

160

not our problem.'

'So which setting are the Blakelys claiming for?'

Cass gave him a bewildered look. 'They can't claim for anything, can they? Not if they get the necklace back.'

Noel was about to reply when his mobile phone started to buzz. He watched her taking a file out of her desk while he listened to what Kevin was telling him. It wasn't good news, but Cass needed to know.

'That was one of my junior detectives. Dempsey is in Norton hospital. He's been beaten up rather badly.'

Cass pressed her lips together. 'I knew I should have given him the necklace. He got attacked because he didn't have the sapphires. Does Rachel know?'

'Do you want me to notify her?'

She shook her head. 'Not yet. I need to find out how bad he is first. I want to talk to him. I bet this wasn't a random attack. If I'd given him the necklace when he came to the studio, he wouldn't be in hospital.'

'You're not going anywhere near Dempsey. I'm going to see him as soon as I leave here. He will have told his attackers about you, Cass, so they'll know exactly where to find the sapphires. I'll take the necklace back to Norton and put it in the police safe.'

She gave him a cool look. 'Yeah, that's a brilliant idea. So if the thugs come after me looking for the sapphires, I won't have them either, and I'll finish up in a bed next to Dempsey. I'd rather hand them over and maybe avoid getting beaten up.'

She was right, of course. If there had been time he might have been able to arrange for a substitute necklace, but he doubted a substitute would have fooled the smugglers for long. The way things stood at the moment, he was pretty sure the thieves would be calling on Cass quite soon. He needed time to think. Time to work out how to keep Cass and her mother safe.

She handed him a sheet of paper.

'That gives you the weight and size of each sapphire, and I still have the pieces of the original setting.' She opened her safe to take out a small plastic bag. 'You said the broken bits of metal might tell you where it was made.'

He *had* said that; he remembered saying it, and he should have sent the pieces off to be analysed days ago. Working next to Cassandra Moon addled his brain. She turned to look at him as if she had read his thoughts. Her eyes were amazing. He'd noticed that before. Clear blue sometimes, but now almost lilac, set in a perfect oval face framed with a fall of burnished copper hair. He must have moved towards her because she stopped him with a hand on his chest.

'Don't push your luck.'

'Sorry, Cass. It's not just electricity, it's some sort of magnetism. And that's not a euphemism — I mean it seriously.'

'I know. Do you think I don't feel it too? But it isn't real. It has something to do with all that psychic mumbo-jumbo my mother is always going on about. It has nothing to do with how we really feel about one another.'

He could argue about that, but perhaps not today. 'What's wrong, Cass? I know something's bothering you, and it hasn't anything to do with the sapphires, has it?'

'I haven't had much sleep,' she said, rubbing a hand across her face. 'And that has nothing to do with the sapphires, either. My father wants to meet me.'

'Why?' he blurted before he could stop himself. He knew Cass hadn't seen her father since she was a kid. As far as he knew she didn't even remember him. At one time she had thought he was dead.

She shook her head. 'I have no idea why he wants to see me. My mother has photos of me with him when I was a child, right up until I went to school, but I don't remember anything about him. She says it's because he didn't want me to remember, but he couldn't really do that, could he? Take away my memories?'

The look in her eyes was part fear and part bewilderment, and he wanted to take her in his arms and comfort her. Instead he took her hand in his. 'I can be with you, if you like, when he comes to see you. Moral support and all that. He's not dangerous, Cass. Your mother wouldn't let him near you if he was.'

'I know.' She dropped down onto her swivel chair and spun in a slow circle. 'But he wants to see me for a reason, and I don't know what that reason is — I think it has something to do with the black cat.'

He let go of her hand. 'What has your father got to do with the hellcat? I don't understand.'

'Neither do I! That's just the point!'

She turned away from him angrily, and he wished he hadn't let go of her hand. There were so many things going on that neither of them understood, it was no wonder she was confused and frustrated.

'I'll go and see Dempsey,' he said, hoping a change of subject would help. 'He'll either clam up completely because he's afraid of what might happen to him next time they catch up with him, or he'll talk his pretty little head off. Either way, we've got him where we can keep an eye on him.'

'Are you going to tell Rachel what's going on, or pretend her boyfriend got attacked for no reason at all?'

'It depends whether Dempsey told his muggers about her. That's one of the things I intend to ask him.'

'He cares about her,' Cass said. 'He won't want her to get hurt.'

Noel bent down so he could look deep into those strange lavender eyes. 'Now you know exactly how I feel.' He pressed his lips to her forehead, feeling the tiny spark of electricity right down to his toes. 'I want to keep you safe, Cass, but at the moment I don't know how.' He walked to the door. 'I don't think they'll come for the sapphires tonight, but I'll put a police car at the end of your drive. It might be a bit of a deterrent.' He let himself out — wishing he could do more, hoping he could do enough.

Noel went back to Norton police station before he went to the hospital. The first thing he did was arrange for a car to sit outside Abracadabra all night. He asked them to watch out for the black cat as well; he didn't want anyone opening the gate for that thing again. Once that was organised, he called Kevin into his office and handed the young policeman the bits of metal Cass had given him.

'This is the setting the sapphires were in when they came through customs. I want to know if there's anything unusual about the metal, anything that will help us trace the supplier. I also need to catch Mr Blakely at home and get him to fax me details of the missing sapphires, but the damned time difference is making things difficult. His wife said he doesn't get home till after 8pm, their time. That's the middle of the night over here.' He looked at his watch. 'And I think I'm already too late to catch him before he leaves home this morning.' He scratched his head. 'Now I'm confusing myself. Get Brenda to sort it out, will you, Kevin? She's good with things like that.'

Pulling on a light jacket, he got in his car and headed off for the hospital.

Christopher Dempsey was in a sorry state. His face was a strange colour and an even stranger shape. One eye was completely closed and the other a thin red slit. His mouth looked as if he had been given Botox by a mad scientist, and his lips bristled with the spiky ends of random black stiches. One arm was in a sling and one leg hung from a hoist. He look like one of Dr Frankenstein's failures, Noel thought as he walked towards the bed. Chris probably wasn't very pleased to see him, but it was difficult to tell. Noel pulled up a chair and sat down.

'I don't suppose you can speak, but I've been told you can nod your head. I know we've met before, but I didn't introduce myself properly last time. My name is Noel Raven and I'm the detective inspector at Norton police station. I don't take prisoners. If I don't like you I'll throw you back out there and the gang you're involved with can finish you off. At the moment you're probably as safe as you'll ever be and, if you're a really good boy, we might be able to come to the sort of arrangement that means you don't die of old age while you're still in prison.'

Noel didn't get much of a reaction, but he wasn't expecting one. Much of a reaction wouldn't have been possible, not with the way Dempsey was trussed up. He was happy to settle for the look of resignation in the only visible eye.

'Did you tell your attackers about Rachel?'

The head shake was small but unmistakably negative. Good. At least the man was willing to communicate. Noel metaphorically rolled up his sleeves. Now they could get on to the important stuff.

'Did you tell them where the sapphires are being kept?'

This time it was a nod, but Noel had been expecting that, too.

'Are your mates going to try and get them back?'

When Dempsey didn't move his head at all, Noel frowned. What did that mean?

'Are you trying to tell me you don't know?'

This time the nod was more definite, which was a pity. Noel had been hoping for a date and time, but perhaps that was wishful thinking. He stared into the half-open eye. 'You know they won't give up on this until they get the stones back.'

The silence was palpable. Dempsey didn't move a muscle, but he didn't have to. The eye gave it away. The man was still scared silly. Noel bent down over the bed until he could look into that silver of bloodshot eye.

'Then you're best off in here, aren't you? I wouldn't fancy your chances outside.'

170

A nurse came in to give Dempsey more medication, and Noel wondered if he should put someone outside the room to keep watch; but Dempsey had already been punished for his wrong-doings, so he was probably safe in the hospital. The problem was, they were now going after the necklace. Cass had promised to hand it over if necessary to save her own skin, but he wasn't sure she would keep that promise. He knew how obstinate she could be at times.

171

9

Cass telephoned Liz and asked her friend if she felt like going out for a drink later that evening; she needed to get out of the house for a while. The hellcat was gone — her mother was sure about that — so there was nothing keeping her inside any longer. Liz was on a short shift and would be finished by eight, so she agreed to meet Cass at their usual wine bar.

At least she wasn't likely to bump into Noel, Cass thought as she eased her way past the crowded tables. The wine bar was quite classy; not his cup of tea, probably. She had so much to tell her friend she didn't know where to start. She waited until they were seated, a glass of Chardonnay in front of each of them.

'My mother bought a cat,' she said, deciding to start with something safe. 'I know you said you don't particularly like cats, but Tobias is rather gorgeous.'

Liz opened her eyes wide. 'Dora bought a cat? Why? If she wanted a familiar I would have thought she would have got one long before now.'

'She did have a cat, but it died. I think she must have been quite upset at the time and that's why she didn't get another one. It must have happened some time ago, because I don't ever remember a cat in the house.'

Liz looked at her curiously. 'How far back *can* you remember, Cass? You don't remember your father, even though he must have been around at some point, and now you don't remember the cat. Did something happen when you were a child, something that made you forget everything? A trauma of some sort?'

Cass closed her eyes. She might have guessed no subject was safe with Liz. 'My mother told me my father *made* me forget.'

'Oh, Cass, how awful. What did he do to you? You need to see a counsellor.'

Cass managed a laugh, but stopped before it turned into a sob. 'Nothing. At least, none of the things you might be thinking. He didn't want me to remember him for some reason, and it must have worked because I don't remember him. I just feel kind of sad, I suppose. Because I think he forgot about me, as well. Until a couple of days ago, anyway. Now he wants to see me.'

'He wants to see you?' Liz looked dumfounded. 'But I thought your father was dead.'

'I think my mother contacted him about the cat, and he said he wants to see me. She was as surprised as you are.'

Liz closed her eyes for a moment. 'That is not possible. No one could be as surprised as I am. Nothing you're saying tonight is making any sense at all. What has your father got to do with the new cat? Does he breed them? Sell cats on a market stall? You said he was a sailor. Is it a ship's cat?'

Cass was laughing now. Liz was always good for her. 'Now you're getting silly.'

Liz looked at her in disbelief. '*I'm* getting silly? I can't believe you said that. If this was a contest in silliness, I know who'd win.'

'It's too long a story to go into it all now. My father is coming to see me but I really don't want to see him. Why would I? He's never bothered about me before. I don't know him, I never have known him, so why would I want to see him?'

Liz raised an eyebrow. 'So what are you going to do about it? Go into hiding, or leave the country?'

Cass scowled. 'Something like that. Other things have happened as well. Besides our cat nearly killing that black hellcat, Rachel's boyfriend got beaten up and finished up in hospital. I don't know how bad he is.'

'Oh, poor Rachel. She told me they were coming to see you to pick up the necklace. When did this happen? Was it a robbery, or what?'

Cass hated all the secrecy. She really didn't want to lie, but she didn't want to say anything that might upset Noel's investigation, either. 'I don't know all the details,' she said truthfully. 'Noel just told me he was trying to get hold of Rachel to tell her Dempsey was in hospital.'

'So she may not know anything about it. She was on a long day today, a thirteen-hour shift, so she'll only just be getting home. Should I call her and tell her?'

'No,' Cass said, trying not to sound panicky. 'I'll text Noel and tell him Rachel should be home by now. He's the one with all the information, like how bad Dempsey is and all that. We don't want to upset Rachel if there's no need.' She pulled her phone out of her bag before Liz could disagree, and sent a text to Noel. They barely had time to order another drink before Noel texted her back.

Where are you?

She felt like saying 'none of your business' but there was no point in being deliberately rude; Noel was better at that than she was. She ignored his text and shut down her phone. She wanted to enjoy an evening with her friend in their favourite bar. She told Liz about the cat fight; how Tobias had been the hero of the night in spite of getting injured quite badly. 'You'll have to come and meet him,' she said. 'My mother is really proud of him.'

'I'll walk back with you,' Liz said. 'I can get a taxi from your house. It won't cost any more than getting one from here, and it's a lovely evening.'

'There's a car following us,' Liz said worriedly when they were about half-way back. 'It's driving very slowly without any lights. Do you think you should call Noel on your mobile?'

Cass glanced behind and then stopped moving. 'Damn the man! It *is* Noel, Liz. I won't have him following me around. He's behaving like a stalker and I shall tell him so.' She stood still and waited until he pulled up beside her. Then she waited while he rolled down his window. 'What the devil do you think you're doing, Noel? You have no right to stalk me.'

'I think I do, actually. I've been to the hospital and Dempsey isn't a pretty sight.' He glanced at Liz. 'Hi, Liz. I managed to get hold of Rachel and she's off to the hospital right now. Perhaps you could give her a call later on and see how she is. She's going to get one hell of a shock when she sees her boyfriend.'

'What happened?' Liz asked. 'Cass said he was attacked.'

'I told Liz I didn't have any details,' Cass said quickly. 'Just that Dempsey had been attacked. Presumably it was a robbery. Did they take his money or watch or anything?' She didn't want Noel to think she had blabbed to Liz about the sapphires.

'I don't have any details myself at the moment. The man can't speak. He has a broken arm, torn tendons in his leg, and his face is a mess; but according to his doctor, he should make a full recovery. He might not look quite as pretty in future,' Noel added, 'but that's the least of his worries.'

Cass tried to ignore the lack of concern in his voice. Sometimes Noel Raven wasn't a very nice man. 'I'll go and see him tomorrow. I've met him and I'd feel bad if I didn't.'

'I'm on duty,' Liz added, 'so I can pop in as well. Why can't he speak?'

Noel shrugged. 'There were a lot of stiches in his lips. Maybe they sewed his mouth shut. Get in the car, girls. I'll run you home.'

'No thank you,' Cass said before Liz could say anything. 'We're enjoying the walk. There have been no signs of muggers or black cats, so I think we're safe for the rest of the way. Liz is coming in to meet Tobias and then she's getting a taxi, so you don't have to worry about either of us, but thank you for your offer.' She smiled to herself when she saw the annoyance on the detective's face. He really didn't like anyone going against him.

'Fine.' He gave Liz a curt nod and rolled his window back up. If there had been gravel on the road it would have made a noise as he drove away.

Liz laughed and linked her arm with Cass. 'Wow, you really like poking at snakes, don't you?'

'He's not a snake, he's a raven,' Cass answered. 'The most he can do is peck at me.'

When they got to the end of the drive, Cass wondered if she had been too hasty in sending Noel away. The drive was dark and the bushes rustled as they passed by. Even Liz looked spooked by the time they reached the gates.

'We should get a light for the drive,' Cass said to her mother once they were safely inside the house. 'It's too dark at the end of the drive.'

Dora said hello to Liz before she replied. 'It can't be done, Cassie. Something to do with drain pipes and electricity. Besides, the black cat has gone. You're safe enough now.'

Surely if her mother could cool a room without air-conditioning, she could manage a little thing like a light at the end of the drive. 'You're always saying you're a witch, Mother; can't you conjure up a little light when we need it?'

Dora smiled. 'You know it's not that easy, Cassie. I'm getting older and my spells are getting weaker. Besides, a ball of light with no visible means of support would mean no tradesmen would come near the house.'

Cass didn't like to think of her mother getting older. With her floss of silver hair and brightly coloured caftans, Dora still looked young and pretty. Would she eventually turn into an old crone and wear a pointy hat?

Liz had found Tobias, and he was lapping up all the attention. He arched his back and practically smiled when Liz tickled him under the chin. His wound had begun to heal nicely and his fur was growing back where Dora had shaved it off. Apart from a missing claw, which Cass hoped was still stuck in the hellcat's skin, he looked almost as good as new.

'He's beautiful,' Liz said. 'I wish I could have a cat, but it wouldn't be fair. I'd have to leave him on his own too much.'

'Some cats don't mind being left alone,' Dora said, 'as long as you get an adult cat and give it lots of love when you are there. Do you want me to see what I can do? I know a woman who runs a cat rescue centre.'

'Do you really think I could have a cat of my own?' Liz asked hopefully, her face lighting up. 'It would be lovely to have someone waiting for me when I come home after a long shift.'

Dora smiled at her. 'I'm sure I can help you find a suitable animal.'

Liz stayed for another glass of wine and then said she had better be going. Cass phoned for a cab and walked with Liz to the end of the drive.

'We'll stay inside the gate until the taxi turns up.' She was still worried about the hellcat, or maybe something even worse, lurking in the bushes. 'That's the tree where the catfight started,' she told Liz, pointing to the gnarled branches of the old oak. There was thick cloud cover tonight, but she would never forget the night of the full moon, with the tree in silhouette and the black cat perched high in its branches. She latched the gate after Liz had gone and walked quickly back to the house, wondering if she would ever feel really safe.

* * *

Noel was too cross with Cassandra to drive straight home. He had been trying to help; trying to stop her getting beaten up because she still had the sapphires. He should have taken them away from her, but he still wasn't sure of the best way to keep her safe. At least if someone came looking for the stones,

183

she had some bargaining power. It annoyed him that he had to worry about her all the time. It distracted him, and he couldn't afford to be distracted.

He wasted a couple of hours at the pub and then went home, intending to go to bed, but once back in his flat he felt too wound up to sleep. He kept thinking of Cass and her mother alone in that big house. If they were relying on a magic spells and a ginger cat to keep them safe, it might not be enough.

In the end, he changed into jeans and a dark sweater and went to check on his surveillance team. He found the car near the end of the drive leading up to the house. It was almost midnight, and everything was quiet and still. The dark grey unmarked police car was hidden in the shadow of some bushes. It had its lights turned off, and was almost impossible to see unless you were looking for it. Anyone else might have thought the two men were doing a good job, but Noel wasn't happy. He parked his own car where it couldn't easily be seen and made his way silently over to the police car. He tapped sharply on the window and frowned when both men jumped like startled deer.

He had picked his two men with care, choosing an older police officer who had been with Norton police for years, and Kevin, whom he knew he could trust. Bill Bloss was sitting in the driver's seat — a good officer, but unambitious, preferring regular hours without too much excitement. Kevin was in the passenger seat, doing his first all-night surveillance since he had become a detective.

The older man rolled down his window and looked sheepishly at Noel. 'We were watching the house. Didn't see you coming.'

'No, I gathered that.' Noel climbed into the back of the car and shut the door, waiting for both men to turn round in their seats and look at him. He peered between them down the drive. 'I wonder that you can see the house. I can't, and my eyes are usually quite good.'

'No one can get past us, sir,' Kevin volunteered. 'It's the only way in and out.'

'By car it is, but if I wanted to get into that house I'd leave my car way back somewhere and go the rest of the way on foot. Maybe sneak through the front garden and go round the back where no one's expecting me.' He leaned back in his seat. 'Why did you park way up here?' He was pretty sure he already knew the answer.

When neither of the men said anything, he helped them out. 'Because the house is haunted, isn't it? Two witches live there and either one of them could put a spell on you. Maybe turn you into a frog. Do you know how ridiculous that sounds? If one of those women got murdered, is that what you'd tell the tribunal?'

Almost on cue, an unearthly howl issued from the bottom of the drive, followed by a deep-throated growl that couldn't possibly have been made by anything human.

To give him his due, Kevin was fast out of the car. He beat Noel in the race down the drive. As they got closer to the house they could hear panicky shouts and a lot of crashing around in the bushes. Noel let Kevin go ahead of him. Youth before beauty was definitely better in this sort of situation. They both arrived at the front gate in time to see two figures disappearing round the back of the house.

'Go left!' Noel shouted to Kevin. Running to the right, he fought his way through thick undergrowth and almost caught up with the fleeing figures. He was a few seconds too late to stop them jumping into a parked four-by-four, but as he ran the last few yards towards the off-roader, Bill came screeching round the corner in the police car and blocked the men's escape route. Noel slowed his pace to a walk. He was out of breath, and the men hadn't got anywhere to go. Show over.

Except it wasn't.

The man in the driver's seat slammed

187

the four-by-four into reverse and headed backwards towards Noel at full speed. He managed to leap to one side, but he had forgotten the all-terrain vehicle could go backwards almost as fast as it could go forwards. The thick under-growth wasn't going to slow it down. The men were getting away, and there wasn't anything he could do about it. As the big car swerved past him he slammed his hand against the driver's door, put-ting every ounce of his anger and frustration into the blow. As he turned away in disgust, the engine stopped and the car came to an abrupt halt.

Noel waited until Kevin caught up with him and Bill climbed out of the police car, and then he opened the driver's door of the four-by-four. The heavily built man inside was desperately trying to restart the engine, but to no avail. The thing was as dead as a corpse. Noel was sure the electrics were fried and the battery probably in need of a trans-plant. He very much doubted it would ever move again. He bent down and stared at the two men inside. They both looked as if they would rather be some-where else — anywhere other than sitting outside a witches' house in the dark. The smell of toasted insulation was making Noel's nose twitch, and the patch of blackened paint on the side of the car would take some explaining, but the job had been completed successfully. Cassandra and her mother were safe.

Noel waited while his officers secured the men and shut them in the back of the police car, and then he walked up to the house.

Tobias met him at the gate. The big cat looked quite pleased with himself.

'You did a good job, Tobias. You managed to sound like a zombie and a werewolf, both at the same time.' Noel looked at the house and saw Cassandra standing just inside the back door. Her hair was mussed, her feet bare, and he thought she looked adorable.

'Who was it?' she asked.

'Two men come to get their stones back. We caught them and they're on

189

their way to our cells right now. It's getting quite crowded in there at the moment.'

'Dora's making tea,' Cass said with a smile. 'Do you want to come in?'

He shook his head. 'No, you have your tea and get back to bed. Give Dora my love.'

As he turned away he thought he heard her whisper, 'Thank you.'

He drove back to his flat wishing with all his heart he could have told her it was all over, but the sapphires were too valuable to leave to idiots like those two. The next thug they sent would be more experienced.

10

The next few days passed uneventfully for Cass. Rachel was so involved with the injured Christopher Dempsey that the necklace was the last thing on her mind, but Cass fixed the new clasp before she locked the sapphires away in her safe. She didn't like leaving a job half-done.

Noel had managed to talk her out of her proposed visit to the hospital, but she still wouldn't let him have the necklace. She was convinced she would be in even more danger if her bargaining power were taken away. She had promised to try and get a message to Noel if the criminals turned up, and he had set up a panic button on her mobile phone.

'One press and I'll be there,' he said. 'They'll come at night again, if they come at all, but I can be with you in minutes.' He also had an alarm installed on the safe in her office. 'I know you need to get in and out of the safe in the daytime, but turn the alarm on when you lock up for the night. It'll make a noise like the *Queen Mary* docking on your doorstep and scare the hell out of them, which will give you time to phone me.'

He made it sound as if Cass was all he was worried about, but she knew him too well. He wanted to catch the men behind the smuggling racket. That was all he really cared about.

Tobias had taken to sleeping on her bed on a regular basis, and he made her feel far safer than any amount of alarms and panic buttons. She tried to ignore all thoughts of her father and his imminent visit. Dora hadn't mentioned him again, and Cass wondered if he had changed his mind. She sincerely hoped so. She dreamed of him suddenly appearing in the middle of the room wearing a cloak covered in stars, a wand in his hand and a pointed hat on his head. In her dream he had a long white beard and looked suspiciously like the wizard from *The Sorcerer's Apprentice*.

The weather had changed and there was an autumnal nip in the air, but her studio had been fitted with a large electric radiator and was always warm. She had work that would keep her going for the rest of the day: repairs to some antique jewellery and a headdress to design for a local bride. For some reason Tobias decided he wanted to accompany her into her studio, and she had to be quite firm with him. It was all very well allowing him on her bed at night, but she didn't need him as a constant companion.

'Stay in the kitchen with Dora,' she told him. 'I don't need you with me every minute of the day. I can manage fine on my own.'

He protested with a yowl and tried rubbing round her legs, but she refused to let him win her over. He was getting like Noel, another bossy male who expected to have his own way all the time. She shut the door, leaving him sitting outside.

She wished she could just put everything else out of her mind and get on with her work, but she kept thinking of Rachel. The poor woman had no idea her new love was a criminal who was likely to spend some time in prison. Cass had no idea what would become of the necklace once the gang had been caught. It certainly wouldn't go back to Rachel, but whatever happened she still had to replace the clasp. And she couldn't stall Rachel forever.

She got the new clasp out of the drawer and went over to the cupboard that housed her safe, then turned the alarm off. Just as she was about to key in the combination, someone knocked on the outside door. Cass looked up in surprise. She wasn't expecting any visitors, and hoped it wasn't Rachel calling to pick up her necklace.

The man standing on her doorstep was well over six feet tall and well-built. He wore a smart business suit buttoned over a broad chest, and would have been quite nice-looking if it wasn't for a scar on his cheekbone. He smiled at her with even white teeth. 'Miss Moon? My name is Robert Finchley and I've called about a sapphire necklace I believe you have.'

She stared at him, frowning. 'I'm sorry? What sapphire necklace?' She was beginning to get a nasty feeling in the pit of her stomach. Apart from the smugglers, no one knew the stones were sapphires except Noel and her mother.

Before she could stop him, the man pushed past her into the studio. He stood still for a moment, looking around. 'Nice. A proper little workplace you've got here. Be a shame if it got messed up. Get the necklace for me, Miss Moon, and I'll be on my way.'

Her phone was on the workbench under the window and she had turned the safe alarm off. She cursed Noel for assuming her visitor would come at night, but cursing Noel wouldn't help. Getting out of this was going to be up to her. She started moving towards the door into the house. Tobias was on the other side of that door and she could do with his help right now.

'I wouldn't if I were you.' He said it casually enough, but the underlying menace made her shiver. 'The stones don't belong to you, so just hand over the necklace and there won't be any trouble.'

'I can't hand anything over without a letter of authority. And I'll need proof of your identity and an official receipt from the rightful owner.' She thought she'd have a go at throwing officialdom at him. 'You must realise I can't just give the necklace to you. You could be anybody.'

'Please, Miss Moon. I can assure you I'm not just anybody. Do what I tell you, OK? It's not worth arguing with me. I'm going to take the necklace whatever you do. I don't want to hurt you, but I can.' He proved his point by giving her a hard slap round the face that nearly knocked her over. 'Open

196

your safe, give me the stones, and I'll get out of your life.'

Cass felt blood in her mouth and realised she'd bitten her tongue. She reached into a box of tissues on the bench and pulled one out. For once, she wished she had taken the judo lessons Liz had suggested. 'I need to put in the combination for the safe,' she said, picking up the alarm keypad.

He took it out of her hand. 'We both know that will set off an alarm and we don't want that, do we? It might upset the neighbours.'

This time he used the back of his hand and the slap literally made her see stars. She staggered, clutching the edge of the workbench for support. The man was a bully and she didn't like bullies. His hand had caught her on the side of her face and she knew she was going to have a black eye, but at least he hadn't broken her cheekbone. A quick inspection with her tongue proved her teeth were all still intact. That was a bonus.

Knowing she had to do something,

she wondered if she dare reach for her phone, but he saw where she was looking and knocked the phone contemptuously off the bench, grinding it under his foot. 'Just open the safe, there's a good girl.'

This time she did as she was told.

The necklace felt cold. Unnaturally cold. Reluctantly, she lifted it out of the safe and carried it to the workbench. Robert Finchley was going to walk away with the necklace, and there wasn't anything she could do about it. At that moment a ray of sun from the open window sent shimmers of light dancing on the ceiling: a multitude of different colours caused by the facets in the stones. The man reached out his hand but hesitated before he touched the necklace.

'Do they always do that?'

'When the sun catches them, yes,' Cass said, but she had never seen that sort of luminosity before, even from the very best gems. Her face still hurt and she didn't owe him any favours, but she thought she probably ought to warn him. 'I wouldn't touch the necklace if I were you,' she said.

He gave her a contemptuous look and took a small bag out of his pocket. She watched as he picked up the necklace and attempted to drop it into the bag, but it didn't immediately leave his hand. He turned to stare at her, a look of surprise on his face. He shook his hand violently and the necklace fell to the ground.

'It burnt me!'

She bent down and picked up the necklace. Finchley was trying to uncurl his fingers, one at a time, obviously in a lot of pain. But she didn't care about his hand, or his pain. The only thing on her mind was the fact that he was no longer watching her.

She lunged for the door and grabbed the handle, pulling it open. Tobias shot into the room, but Finchley wasn't interested in the cat. He kicked the door shut and started towards her at a run, a murderous look on his face.

'Silly bitch! You aren't going any-where.'

Tobias hardly seemed to move, but somehow he became entangled in Finchley's legs. Unable to slow his forward momentum, Finchley tripped over the cat and pitched forward. He was a big man and he fell hard, cracking his head on the edge of Cass's desk before he hit the floor.

For a moment Cass stood looking at him. He was lying very still, and for all she knew he might be dead, but right that minute she didn't care. If he had managed to get to her *she* would probably be dead by now.

The big gold cat was looking at her expectantly and she ran a hand down his glossy back, thanking him for his help.

After a few seconds she squatted down beside Finchley and felt for a pulse. She was glad when she found it. Not because the man was still alive, but because she wouldn't get done for murder. She turned his hand over and looked at the burn on his palm. She could see what appeared to be a deep hole, the edges blistered and singed. Whatever it was, it would take some explaining if they had to call a doctor. Calling Noel seemed like a better idea, but her phone was lying on the floor in pieces, and setting off the safe alarm would be a bit pointless.

She was just wondering if she dare leave Finchley on his own while she fetched her mother, when Dora walked into the room. She looked at the man on the floor. 'What happened, Cassie?'

'I had a visitor,' Cass said shakily. She was having her first-ever panic attack. Her chest felt too tight to take a breath and her whole body was shaking. She knew she had to pull herself together, but she had no idea how. Dora took hold of her hands and she felt the shaking stop. Perhaps in a few minutes she would be able to breathe again.

'I don't know what happened,' she gasped out at last. 'He picked up the necklace and said his hand was burning. I managed to open the door and Tobias tripped him up. He hit his head on my desk. He's still got a pulse, so he's not dead.'

Dora got down on her knees beside the man. She reached out and gently uncurled his fingers, exposing a black mark in the centre of his palm. The edges looked blistered. 'His hand wasn't burned with heat, Cassie. It looks like a severe case of frostbite.'

Cass picked up the necklace. It was cool, but not cold, and the stones no longer sparkled with the same brilliance as they had earlier. 'Can you help him?' she asked her mother. 'Or should we call an ambulance?'

Dora got to her feet. 'What are you going to tell the paramedics? It's hardly the middle of winter. I've already called Noel. He will want to speak to this man before anyone else does.'

Noel arrived at a run, bursting into the room like a tornado. 'The kitchen door was unlocked. What happened?'

'I don't know,' Cass said before Dora

could answer. She nodded towards the man. 'His name is Finchley. At least, that's what he told me. He came looking for the sapphires and I handed them over like you told me to, but then something happened. His hand has been burned, Noel. He has frostbite.'

Noel looked at Dora. 'How on earth did he get frostbite? It's almost seventy degrees outside.'

Dora shook her head. 'I have no idea. If you keep an eye on him I'll get something to stop the pain in his hand. He's really going to feel it when he comes round. Not that he deserves any help. I think he hit Cassie. She's got a bruise on her face.'

Noel's eyes darkened. 'Did he hurt you?'

Cass put a hand to her face. 'Not much. Not as much as I hurt him. We really do need to call an ambulance, or at least a doctor. His hand looks really bad and he's still unconscious.' Cass wished she had been more forceful when she told Finchley not to touch the necklace. She had known something bad was going to happen.

Finchley moaned and tried to sit up. His eyes looked unfocused, and there was blood running down the side of his face.

'I think he's got concussion.' Noel reached into a back pocket and pulled out a pair of plastic ties.

Cass looked at him in disbelief. 'He's badly hurt, Noel. You can't tie his hands together.'

'I don't intend to tie his hands together. Not yet.' He bent down beside Finchley and anchored his good hand to the leg of the desk, then proceeded to secure the man's ankles with another tie. 'He's going to wake up properly in a minute and he's not going to lie there like a lamb. He's hurting, and he's going to want to hurt someone back. That's the nature of people like him.'

'You're generalising,' Cass said, but when Finchley groaned again and pushed himself into a sitting position, the focus was back in his eyes, and she knew Noel had been right.

'I'm a policeman,' Noel told the groaning man. 'If you move even the tiniest bit, I will tie both your hands together, and that will hurt a lot.'

Dora came back into the room carrying a covered basket. 'I can fix the cut on his head and take away most of his pain, but he needs more treatment than I can give him here. You can't lock him up until he's seen a doctor, so he's going to have to go to hospital eventually.'

Finchley started to say something but stopped when Noel walked towards him. 'I really want to hurt you for what you did to Cass, so I should keep still and shut up if I were you.'

Dora took a bottle out of her basket and poured the liquid into one of Cass's mugs. 'I finally found a use for the mandrake,' she said with a smile. 'I don't like wasting things.' She handed Finchley the mug. 'Drink it all and it will take most of your pain away. Once it starts working, I'll be able to dress your hand.'

Within minutes the man had stopped

making any noise at all. When Dora told him to, he obediently held out his injured hand. She looked at the burn and pulled a face. 'I'll do what I can, but he's always going to have a scar. Put the necklace back in your safe for the time being, Cass. We don't want anyone else getting hurt.'

'Are you telling me it was the necklace that did that to his hand?' Noel asked in disbelief.

Dora started smearing pink cream over Finchley's palm. 'It was protecting Cassie. He was hurting her, and she couldn't call anyone because he'd broken her phone.'

'And because you told me no one would come for the sapphires in the daytime, I'd turned off the alarm on the safe.' Cass bent down beside her mother, wincing at the sight of Finchley's hand. 'Am I responsible for that?'

Dora undid a roll of bandage. 'Probably. You need to learn how to control your power, Cassie, but this time it saved you.'

'I gave him the stones. That was all he wanted. He would have gone and left me alone. I didn't need any help.'

'Maybe the stones thought otherwise,' Noel said. 'It wasn't your fault, Cass. You had no control over any of this.'

'Exactly,' Dora said. 'That's what I've been trying to tell her.' She finished binding the man's hand and then fitted his arm into a roughly made sling. 'I didn't give you enough of a sedative to knock you out,' she told Finchley. 'You deserve to suffer a bit. You'll be back to normal in a few minutes and your hand will start hurting again.'

He looked up at her blearily. 'What did you give me? You've no right to drug me without my permission. It's against the law.'

Noel let out a hoot of laughter and snapped a tie back on Finchley's wrist, anchoring it to the handle of Cass's filing cabinet. 'There is only one law around here, Mr Finchley, and that's me.' He looked at Dora and smiled with satisfaction. 'Now you can call an ambulance if you want to.'

'What are you going to tell the paramedics when they get here?' Dora asked. 'They'll want to know how he got that burn on his hand.'

'What could cause a burn like that?' Noel asked. 'Something electrical?'

'The necklace was freezing cold,' Cass said. 'Finchley has frostbite, like you get in the Arctic.'

'Dry ice?' Dora suggested. 'Suppose there were some pellets of dry ice lying around and he picked them up? If he held them in his hand long enough he would get a burn like that.'

'Dry ice it is, then.' Noel said. 'Cass was using the pellets in an experiment, something to do with her jewellery, and when Finchley got hurt she called me because I've been working on this case. When I got here, I cautioned the man and then immobilised him in case he was dangerous.'

'Not yet, you haven't,' Finchley muttered. The potion Dora had given him had worn off and he was beginning to think for himself again. 'You haven't cautioned me, or read me my rights. And I shall tell the paramedics what really happened. You can't stop me telling the truth.'

'I wouldn't dream of trying to stop you telling the truth,' Noel said with a smile, 'but who do you think is going to believe you? Are you trying to get off with an insanity plea? Because you might just succeed.'

'I didn't touch any dry ice.' Finchley glared at Cass. 'You did something to those stones and they burnt my hand. You're making things up that never happened.'

Cass bent down and glared back. 'So what did happen, exactly? You broke in to my studio and tried to steal a necklace I was repairing for a client. I have a bruise to prove it. Then what happened? Why don't you tell everyone the truth, Mr Finchley? I really don't mind.'

Dora finished packing her basket. 'I'll let the paramedics in when they get here. We'll see if they drive right up to the house or stop at the end of the drive.' She smiled at Finchley. 'Like you said, Mr Finchley, we are witches and we put spells on people, so most of them are afraid to come right up to the house.'

The handover went without a hitch. The doctor in charge asked if he could have a sample of the dry ice, but Cass told him she'd only had a few pellets and they had turned to vapour in Finchley's hand. 'That's probably why he's a bit incoherent,' she added. 'The vapour from dry ice can be as dangerous as the ice itself.'

Noel explained that Finchley was a criminal involved in an ongoing smuggling case and he would need to accompany the injured man to the hospital. Finchley was loaded into a wheelchair and Noel fastened him securely for the drive to hospital. He told Cass he'd be in touch later in the evening.

By the time she had locked up the studio and walked to the kitchen, Dora already had a pot of tea standing on the table. It smelt a little odd and Cass wondered what her mother had added to the pot this time, but she decided she didn't really care. She still felt shaky, her face still hurt, and now she was tired and hungry.

'Tea first,' Dora said, 'and then you can tell me exactly what happened.' She handed Cass a tiny tube of cream. 'Put some of that on your face. If you don't, you'll have a black eye. Dinner will be ready in about ten minutes.' She smiled as she refilled Cass's cup. 'The ambulance stopped at the top of the drive, so they had to push that heavy wheelchair over all those bumps and potholes. Some people are very odd, aren't they?'

Cass nodded. You could say that. The cream her mother gave her took away the ache and the tea settled her nerves. Sometimes she was quite glad her mother was a witch. And yes, Dora was quite right; other people are often very odd.

Dora listened to Cass's account of the man's appearance in the studio in silence. 'So you knew something bad was going to happen to him if he picked up the necklace?' she said when Cass had finished.

'No, of course I didn't. Not for sure. How could I? I just had this gut feeling that he shouldn't touch the sapphires — and I told him not to — but he wasn't listening to me. He just wanted to take the necklace and go. I had no control over any of it.'

'And that's the problem, Cassie. The stones are reacting to your thoughts and emotions, but you have no control over them. You need learn that control. I can't teach you, but I think your father can.'

Cass shook her head. 'That's just silly. He knows nothing about me, nothing about my thoughts and emotions. Besides, I don't believe I had anything to do with what happened today. Finchley just reacted badly to the sapphires — or the gold in the setting.

An allergic reaction, that's all it was.'

'I don't think an allergic reaction can cause a third-degree burn,' Dora said mildly. 'Anyway, your father is already here in town, so you might as well get used to the idea that you'll meet him sometime soon.'

'When?' Cass felt the panic rise inside her like a physical thing, but she wouldn't let it get the better of her this time. She took a couple of deep breaths. 'Do you know when he's coming?'

'No. If he wanted either of us to know he'd tell us. If I had to make a guess, I'd say next Friday.'

'My birthday? Why on earth would he come to see me on my birthday? Not to bring me a present, that's for sure. He hasn't bothered about my birthday since I was born, so why now?'

'He always remembers your birthday, Cassie. You have a bank account with twenty-eight thousand pounds in it. All the money is from your father, but you can't touch it until you're thirty.'

Cass looked at her mother in

complete bewilderment. 'Why didn't you tell me?'

'Because he didn't want me to, which meant I couldn't.'

'What's so special about my thirtieth birthday? Why do I get the money then?'

Dora smiled. 'It's a wedding present.'

11

The drive to the hospital was uneventful, but Noel kept a close eye on Finchley. He needed to get as much information as he could from the man, but Finchley wouldn't be an easy nut to crack even though he wasn't at the top of the chain. Noel knew there were others above him. What was needed was a lever, something to make the man talk; he just hadn't found it yet.

There were two holding cells at Norton police station, both small and cramped and not intended for more than a one-night stay. Most of the occupants were vagrants who needed somewhere to kip down, drunken yobs, or teenaged joyriders. Finchley was probably the first bona fide criminal a Norton cell had ever played host to.

Brenda made sure the cells were spotlessly clean, but they still smelled like the inside of a wheelie bin. The prisoners were provided with a metal bed with a plastic-covered mattress and pillow, a small chair, and an all-in-one toilet and washing facility. The door was heavy metal with a small window of unbreakable glass.

Finchley straightened his tie and brushed down his trousers before he sat gingerly on the edge of the bed. 'You can't hold me,' he said. 'You must know that. Your girlfriend let me in and we had a little chat, then she nearly burned my hand off. It's her that should be in here.'

Noel leaned against the cell wall. 'You don't get a burn like that from just having a chat, do you? You must know that, Mr Finchley. Do you have a plausible explanation worked out that might make sense? Cassandra Moon and her mother have a good story to tell, one that will be believed. About how you forced you way into the studio and tried to steal a necklace. Picking up a handful of dry ice and getting badly burned was entirely your fault.'

Finchley moved on the bed, sitting up a fraction straighter. 'What dry ice? I didn't see any dry ice, and I certainly didn't touch anything like that. I don't even know what it looks like.'

'Exactly,' Noel said with a smile. 'So how do you know you didn't touch any? You might be able to plead that burning yourself with the dry ice was an accident, but the forced entry and attempted burglary was definitely deliberate.' Finchley moved his injured hand, cradling it in his lap, and Noel wondered if it was starting to hurt again. 'It's lucky the older lady is a witch,' he said. 'No one else could have taken your pain away like she did. Her daughter is pretty good at magic spells, as well. How do you think the sapphires got so cold that they gave you frostbite? It doesn't pay to muck about with witches. You might still lose your hand.'

'You're the mad one,' Finchley said with a brave sneer. 'You can't prove anything. It's my word against theirs

217

and, from what I heard, a lot of people in the village think those two women are nuts.'

Someone knocked on the cell door and Noel turned to look through the window. Trevor stood on the other side of the glass, looking apologetic. Noel had given very specific instructions not to be disturbed.

'I'll be back,' he told Finchley, hoping he didn't sound too much like Arnold Schwarzenegger. He let himself out of the cell and frowned at Kevin.

'Sorry, sir. There's a man here who wants to see Finchley. Pulled a bit of rank on Brenda and she said to come and get you.'

'Who is he?'

Kevin looked at the bit of paper he was carrying. 'Henry Moore. Someone really high up in special ops. He works for a department called ITG.'

Noel raised an eyebrow. Just because the letters sounded important it didn't mean they were. 'What the hell is that?'

With another look at his bit of paper,

Kevin said, 'It stands for Illegal Transportation of Gemstones. Moore wants to talk to our prisoner.'

'Damn!' Noel wasn't going to give Finchley up without a fight. 'How did some government department that sounds like a fast food restaurant get involved with my case?' Finchley was peering at him through the glass of his cell window and Noel felt like putting his tongue out at the man. 'What happened to that little shutter you used to be able to pull across to stop prisoners looking out?'

'The human rights crowd stopped that, sir. Every prisoner has to be able to see outside their cell; otherwise they might have a panic attack.'

'It's a cell,' Noel said in exasperation, 'and we never keep anyone longer than one night. They'll want French doors out onto a garden next.' He looked at the man gawping at him through the glass and remembered the reel of sticky tape Brenda used on parcels. A couple of strips of that would do the job. 'OK, take me to this ITG guy and let's see what he wants.'

Brenda had put the man in his office, which didn't please Noel, but the only other place would have been the interview room and that wouldn't have appeared very friendly. No point in getting off on the wrong foot, he supposed.

Henry Moore was about the same height as Noel, but probably at least twenty years older. He was an imposing man with a deeply tanned face who had a rugged look about him, in spite of his smart grey suit and crisp white shirt. His hair was almost black, except for the odd streak of grey, and nearly touched his collar. Noel thought he looked more like an intrepid explorer than a government officer. He held out his hand and Noel took it. The handshake was firm but not intimidating.

'Sorry, I don't know your department. Some government offshoot, I imagine.'

'Not exactly.' The man smiled, and

the sparkling white teeth in that rustic brown face *were* intimidating. 'My department is more covert operations. I work for anyone who requires my services. I don't answer to anyone in particular. However, I don't want to waste your time, so I'll get to the point of my visit. You have a prisoner who belongs to a smuggling organisation we've been following for some months. The man you have in custody is not at the top of the ladder, but far enough up to cause interest. I would like your permission to question this man.'

Not if I can help it, Noel thought, mentally girding his loins for battle. 'I'm sorry, sir, but that is my prisoner and I am quite capable of questioning him myself. If I obtain any information that I think may be of interest to your department, I promise I'll pass it on to you.'

Moore sighed. 'That's not going to happen, Raven. My department is so many rungs up the ladder from your little rural police force you wouldn't be able to spot it through the clouds. I really don't want to pull rank on you, but I will if I have to, and I assure you I can. One phone call from me and your prisoner will be picked up and transported out of your jurisdiction.' He unbuttoned his jacket and sat down on Noel's visitor's chair. 'Or we can be civilized about this and I'll allow you to be present when I question your prisoner.'

There was a knock on the door and Brenda popped her head in. 'Would either of you like a cup of coffee?'

Moore gave her the benefit of his smile. 'That would be lovely, and the timing was very intuitive. I can tell you're a detective. Black for me, please, no sugar.'

Brenda looked as if she might faint with pleasure and Noel rolled his eyes. 'Thank you, Brenda, coffee would be nice. And two sugars for me,' he added perversely. He had been going without sugar to keep his weight down. He knew it was a bit like having a mild tantrum, but he didn't care.

Moore didn't seem keen on small talk, and Noel hoped the coffee would arrive before the silence became embarrassing. After about ten minutes Brenda came in bearing a tray and a bright smile. Noel was pretty sure she had taken the time to re-apply her lipstick. 'I'll leave the pot,' she said, 'in case you want another cup.' She raised an eyebrow when Noel spooned in his sugar, then left the room with another big smile for Moore.

'Nice woman,' Moore said. 'I need to see your case files at some point, Raven. What's Bosco calling himself at the moment? He's got passports for half a dozen identities.'

'Finchley. Educated British accent. Smartly dressed.'

'Tell me what he's been up to. How you came to get involved. I take it the gang slipped up somewhere. Unusual for them, but it had to happen sometime. Law of averages.'

'You could say that. One of their patsies got taken sick at the airport in

Miami and the girl came home all by herself wearing the sapphires.'

'She wasn't in on it?'

'No.'

'So how did you get to arrest Bosco? He's quite a slippery character.'

Noel didn't think he could tell this man the truth and be believed, so he gave the dry ice version that was in his report. 'The young man who bought the necklace in the first place got assaulted by one of the gang. He's still in hospital, but I think he just wanted a pretty necklace for a girl he met on the beach. He told his attackers everything, including the jeweller's address.'

'Your witnesses are all known to you, Raven. Cassandra Moon, her mother, and the woman who brought the necklace through customs — something a lawyer will latch on to. What's your strategy? Were you expecting to get a confession from Finchley?'

'I thought it might be possible. The man was quite badly hurt, but the hospital let him go once they'd patched up his hand. They didn't want a criminal taking up a bed. Finchley had a bad scare and I was going to play on that when I interrogated him.'

Moore sat back in his chair and looked at Noel thoughtfully. 'I didn't think Bosco was a man who would scare easily, but OK, I'll go along with that. You lead the interrogation and I'll interrupt if I feel the need. How does that sound?'

Noel had been going to throw witches and warlocks and magic spells at Finchley, but he couldn't do that with Moore in the room. Then again, Finchley wouldn't want to make a fool of himself by talking about burning sapphires and mandrake potions, so there might be a chance to get something out of him.

By the time they got Finchley into the interview room, he had recovered his nerve. Noel insisted on securing the man's hand to the chair, hoping it might deflate his confidence a little. It would be interesting to see what

Finchley had decided to use as his defence.

'I'm just here as an observer,' Moore said soothingly. 'If you're honest with both of us, I might be able to help you.'

'Fat chance,' Finchley said. 'All I did was call on the woman to pick up a necklace, and she burned my hand down to the bone. She ought to be the one sitting here. She's got a lot to answer for.'

'How exactly did she burn your hand?' Moore asked, sitting forward on his chair. 'Did she make you pick up the ice?'

'I didn't see any ice,' Finchley said sullenly. 'She must have put it in my hand when she handed me the necklace. She burned me deliberately for no reason. I can sue her for that. Get compensation for not being able to use my right hand again.'

'Perhaps Detective Raven knows how Cassandra Moon managed to burn your hand. Would you like to carry on with the questioning, Detective?'

'Cassandra Moon's mother helped you afterwards, didn't she, Finchley? She gave you a sedative to stop the pain, and cleaned the wound and dressed it. She probably saved your hand from amputation.'

'That was no ordinary sedative! She used something that almost made me unconscious. That's the only reason you were able to handcuff me. I don't know what she gave me, but she's a witch; all the people in the village know that.'

Moore looked faintly amused. 'Was that a metaphor, Finchley, or are we to take that as a serious accusation? It won't hold up in court, you know. Witches aren't burned at the stake anymore.' He looked at Noel. 'We're wasting our time here. I think you've got more than enough to keep this man in custody for a few more days, and that should be long enough.'

Noel was dying to ask Moore what he meant. Long enough for what? It would be difficult to get a conviction on what they had. Moore followed him back to the cell and watched while he locked Finchley inside. The man was at the window almost before the door was closed. Noel waited until Moore had his back turned and then he put out his tongue. Childish, he knew, but it made him feel a whole lot better. He led Moore back to his office and found Brenda had refilled the coffee pot. Good. He didn't want Moore to leave straight away; he had a few questions of his own.

'I'm sorry the interview with Finchley wasn't more productive, sir.'

Moore smiled as he poured hot coffee for both of them. 'I think I cramped your style a little, Raven, but all I needed was some extra time. I can get you all the evidence you need to convict Bosco in a couple of days so there was no point in spooking him right now.' He handed Noel a mug of coffee. 'The poor man obviously has a thing about witches. I wonder why that is?'

Noel had a feeling Moore was playing some sort of game with him, but he had no idea what it was. 'Mrs Moon sells recipes for herbal remedies quite legitimately on the internet. She finds having a reputation as a witch quite good for her business, I believe.'

Moore put his head on one side and looked at Noel with a slight smile on his face. 'Are you telling me you don't believe in witches, Raven? I'm surprised. I would have thought you were a man with an open mind.' He pushed his chair back and stood up before Noel could reply. 'I must be going.' He held out his hand. 'I glad I met you, Raven. Hang on to our smuggler for a couple of days. I'll be seeing you again shortly.'

Noel took the proffered hand, shook it briefly, and let go. He still felt part of some game, a game where no one had told him the rules. Moore had his own agenda and wasn't going to give anything away if he didn't have to — the sort of behaviour he had come to expect from someone who worked for an acronym.

He called Brenda to show the man

out, but Moore paused in the doorway. 'Don't try looking for my department online, Raven. We don't exactly advertise ourselves.'

Noel walked to his office window and saw Moore get into his car, a big black saloon that had been parked on double yellows for the last hour. Noel had someone policing those yellow lines 24/7 and Moore should have got a ticket. His department had been trained not to give special treatment to anyone, however high up the pecking order. He phoned downstairs and got their youngest recruit, a young man barely out of his teens who couldn't tell a lie if he tried.

'There's been a big black car parked outside on double yellows for nearly an hour. It's gone now, but you should have given the driver a ticket.'

'What big black car?' the young officer asked, sounding genuinely puzzled.

* * *

Cass asked Rachel round a few days later for coffee. Noel had taken the necklace, but now he wanted the earrings as well. He had left it up to Cassandra to tell Rachel her jewellery was stolen property. There didn't seem to be any way of giving Rachel the news without upsetting her, so Dora had suggested coffee and biscuits in the big kitchen.

Dora wanted to meet Rachel again. Cass had no idea why, but she went along with the idea. It meant the visit would be more informal. She hated being the harbinger bad news, but Noel obviously hated it even more, because he had dumped the whole problem in her lap.

Cass let Rachel through the front door and ushered her into the kitchen. The woman was dressed in skinny black jeans and a pale pink top with long sleeves. She looked positively radiant, which immediately made Cass feel guilty.

Dora was putting biscuits on a flowered plate and she looked up with a smile. 'Hello, Rachel. We didn't get a chance to talk to one another last time we met. I hope you didn't worry too much about letting the black cat into our garden. It wasn't a problem. My big tom cat soon saw it off.'

'Oh, my goodness,' Rachel said, as Tobias stood up and stretched, 'he's as big as a baby tiger. I'm not surprised that little black cat was scared.'

Cass was about to interrupt. Rachel was making Tobias sound like a bully when he was still getting over his wounds, but Dora gave her a warning look and she kept quiet. 'Please sit down, Rachel. I'll pour you a cup of tea. Milk and sugar?' When Rachel nodded, Dora sat down beside her. 'How is that nice young man you were with last time? The police detective seems to think he might be involved in something a little shady, but that doesn't seem likely to me.'

'He believes the necklace you brought through customs may have been stolen,' Cass interrupted quickly. 'He's not suggesting you had anything to do with it, but he hasn't been able to speak to

Christopher because of his injuries. I sure it will all be sorted out. I'm sorry I can't give you back your necklace, but it's going to be needed for evidence. Noel will want your earrings as well, I'm afraid.'

Rachel took a sip of her coffee. 'Please don't worry about it. I haven't paid you anything for your work, and I should have, really, because of all the time you spent resetting the stones. They're real, aren't they? I know that now. As soon as the swelling went down and Chris could speak again, he told me everything. He had no idea the stones were real sapphires when he bought them. He only paid $30 for the necklace, so there was no way he could know, was there?'

Rachel sounded as if she was asking for reassurance and Cass wished Chris Dempsey's story could be true, but she was pretty sure he knew only too well something illegal was going on. As it was, his run of bad luck had actually given credence to his alibi. She hoped

Noel would realise that arresting Dempsey would undermine Rachel's confidence all over again, and she didn't need that. Besides, there was no real evidence to prove him guilty.

'How is Chris?' she asked. 'He's obviously talking again. How long are they going to keep him in hospital?'

'A few more days,' Rachel said. 'I've asked him to come and stay with me when he comes out. He's still going to be on crutches, so he'll need someone to look after him. I really don't mind,' she added quickly when she saw the look on Cass's face. 'He's not taking advantage of me or anything. I have a large two-bedroom flat. I've told him if there's going to be anything between us he's got to take it slowly. He told me he has something very special to give me once he comes out of hospital.' She blushed. 'I won't be rushed into anything, but a long engagement would be fine by me.'

'Do you think that's wise?' Cass asked worriedly.

Dora didn't give Rachel time to answer. 'When that happens, when you've got that ring on your finger, you come right over here and we'll open a bottle of champagne. I always keep a few in the chiller compartment for special occasions.'

Cass stared at Dora's big American-style refrigerator. She had no idea they had a chiller compartment. She was always afraid to look inside because of what she might find. Once, there had been two dead frogs in the ice tray.

12

There was a loud knock that had all three of them turning towards the back door. Noel let himself in before either Cass or her mother could get to it, but he pulled up short when he saw who was sitting at the kitchen table. 'Ah,' he said.

Rachel beamed at him. 'Hello, Detective. I didn't know you were visiting as well. It's lovely to see you again.'

'I've already told Rachel you're going to need the necklace as evidence.' Cass gave him a look that said, *What are you doing here?*

He gave her a big smile and dropped into the spare chair next to Rachel, making Cass the last one standing. She walked across the room and fetched a stool, giving him a withering look. He'd got her to do his dirty work for him and she was managing just fine, so what did he want? Had he come to check on her?

'I'm glad you're here,' Noel told Rachel, turning in his chair so they were face to face, 'because I've got some good news for you. We've got enough evidence to convict the man we have in custody, so we won't be pressing charges against Christopher Dempsey. Once he's well enough to leave hospital, he'll be free to go wherever he likes.'

Rachel threw her arms round Noel and kissed him on the cheek. 'Thank you so much! I knew Chris was innocent.'

Noel knew that was going to happen, Cass thought. That was why he'd sat next to her. And he didn't say Dempsey was innocent, he just said there wasn't enough evidence to charge him, which was slightly different. She found a smile from somewhere and pasted it on her face, wondering why she was feeling so irritable. It *was* good news, after all, and maybe Rachel was one of those touchy-feely people who kissed every-one. Maybe.

Cass looked at Noel and he winked

at her. If her cup hadn't been full of tea, she'd have thrown it at him, saucer and all. She had no idea why he always put her in a bad mood, but he managed it every time. She bit into her biscuit with such force most of it landed in her lap, and that didn't help her mood either.

Noel didn't show any sign of leaving, and Dora kept plying him with tea and biscuits, but Rachel eventually stood up and said Chris would be expecting her for the evening visiting session. 'It's a good thing I work at the hospital,' she said with a happy little smile, 'because it means I can pop in and see him whenever I get a spare minute.'

Noel waited until Cass shut the door on Rachel and turned around. 'She's a nice woman, isn't she, Cass? Very pleasant.'

Cass almost growled, but managed to stop herself. She wasn't jealous. Not the slightest little bit. Why would she be? She took the glass of clear liquid Dora handed her and looked at it suspiciously. 'What's this?'

'Only vodka and tonic,' Dora said soothingly. 'You look as if you need something stronger than tea.'

'It must have been stressful for you.' Noel sounded genuinely concerned. 'I know it was your idea to give her the bad news yourself, but it couldn't have been much fun. I'm glad we don't have enough evidence to convict Dempsey. That way, I don't feel so guilty about taking away her sapphires. What on earth does she see in him? He looks like a beach bum. Some women have no taste.' He took the glass of vodka Dora handed to him and nodded his thanks. 'Mind you, Rachel's not to my taste, either. She'd drive me bonkers in two seconds flat. She's far too gushy and clingy. I prefer my women like you, Cass — always ready for a fight.'

Was that a compliment? Cass sighed. She would never understand Noel Raven. Just when she had convinced herself she really disliked him, he did or said something that changed her opinion. It was all very confusing. She downed her vodka and held out her glass for a refill. He was right, though — it had been a stressful afternoon; but that wasn't what was screwing her up inside. Her father's impending visit was still top of the list.

'We had a visitor at the police station the other day,' Noel said. 'A guy called Henry Moore from some obscure government department involved in the movement of precious stones. I thought he wanted to take over my investigation, but he was quite helpful. He knows about Finchley. The man's a known felon, and once we can pin something definite on him he should go away for a long time.'

'Henry Moore?' Dora said quietly. 'What did this man look like?'

Cass gave her mother a curious look. Dora was standing very still, but Cass could see her hands shaking slightly. Did she think she knew this man?

Noel was looking just as puzzled. 'My height. Late fifties, probably, but still looking good. Dark hair streaked with white, and piercing blue eyes. He's ex-Navy SEAL and looks as tough as nails, as if he could handle most situations without too much trouble. A man I'd want on my side.'

'Hector,' Dora said. 'Hector Moon or Henry Moore. This man is your father, Cassie. He changes his name but not his initials.'

Cass felt the blood drain from her face. 'Are you sure, Mother?' Her heart started to beat faster and she felt a little sick. 'You mean he's here in town?' With a flutter of panic, she realised he could arrive any minute. A man she didn't know and had never met. A man who was supposed to be her father. She looked at Noel, hoping for some support, but he was looking just as bewildered.

'What has your husband got to do with my case?' he asked Dora. 'Is he really employed by the government, or is he lying about that as well as his name?'

Dora sank down into the chair Rachel had recently vacated. 'I have no idea, Noel. Hector thrives on intrigue, so he may well work for some secret service agency. It would suit him very well.'

'But it's my case, damn it! He has no right to interfere with . . . ' Noel stopped mid-sentence. 'But he had the files. He got all the information about the smuggling ring from the agency he works for. He couldn't have made that up.'

'It was my case to start with,' Cass interrupted. 'You wouldn't have known anything about the smuggling gang if it wasn't for me.' She turned to her mother. 'Is that what this is all about? Is that the real reason my father wants to see me? Not because I'm his daughter, but because I'm involved in his investigation?'

Dora shook her head sadly. 'I don't know, Cassie. Your father has never told me the reason for any of his actions. If he *is* part of a government organisation, he will be right at the top. Hector Moon only works for himself.'

Cass got to her feet. 'You realise he

could be knocking on that door any minute, and we have no idea why!' She snorted derisively. 'It's certainly not just to wish me a happy birthday, is it?'

'He's still your father, Cassie. I know he checks every now and again to see what you're doing. He knows you work with precious stones. It could be a coincidence that Hector's case involves your stones.'

Cass snorted again. She was sure she was beginning to sound like a pig. 'Ask Noel what he thinks about coincidences. As far as he's concerned, they don't exist.'

'There's always the exception that proves the rule.' Noel held up his hands in submission when he saw the look on her face. 'No, you're quite right, I don't believe in coincidences. But Rachel didn't bring the sapphires to you because you're Hector Moon's daughter, did she? So if you need answers, you'll have to find out why your father wants to see you. And you'll only find that out by meeting him.'

Cass hated the smug look on Noel's face, but he was right, of course. She had to meet her father face to face.

'He'll be here the day after tomorrow,' Dora said. 'He'll come on your birthday, Cassie.'

'Then you still have two days before his visit.' Noel got to his feet. 'I can't get the boss man myself, because he's probably in the States somewhere and out of my jurisdiction. That's why I need Henry Moore. I'll be here on your birthday, Cass.' He grinned at her. 'It should be quite a party with a witch and a warlock present, not to mention someone who can turn a gemstone into a lethal weapon.'

Dora stood up and walked with him to the door. 'Don't count yourself out, Noel. Your power is dormant most of the time, but you will need to call on it sooner than you think.' When he turned to say something, she shook her head. 'Don't question your power — just accept it. Come back in two days' time and we'll celebrate Cassie's birthday. I think Hector will want you here.'

'Some birthday party,' Cass grumbled as her mother closed the door behind Noel. 'It looks as if Noel and my father will be discussing their smuggling investigation most of the time. I think that's the only reason he's coming here. My birthday is just an excuse.' That scenario made more sense to her. There was no reason for her father to want to come and see her, but if he had found out the missing sapphires were in her possession, then his sudden interest had a plausible explanation. Cass had forgotten the cat was in the room until he jumped from his chair. He stretched, pushing his back legs out behind him, and trembled with the tension in his body. 'We mustn't forget Tobias,' she said.

'Or the black cat.' Dora picked up the empty glasses and put them in the sink. 'I think she's close again. She may be a shape shifter.'

It took a lot of effort, but Cass forced herself not to snort. 'I'm beginning to believe there may be something to this magic lark, but I refuse to believe someone can turn into a cat whenever they feel like it. That black cat is feral, that's all. Tobias saw her off, didn't he? You're not telling me he's really a man in cat's clothing.'

'Oh, do stop it, Cassie,' Dora said crossly. 'You have to open your mind a little. I'm not suggesting she can change whenever she wants to. There have been stories of genetic mutation, but I don't believe them. Shape shifting requires a talisman of some sort, or a spell by a very gifted magician. I have no idea how it works, only that it does. If the black cat came knocking at the door in human form neither of us would recognise her, but Tobias would. Even if she got past the safeguards I've put in, he wouldn't let her into the house.'

'What makes you think she's back in this area? I thought she was long gone, never to be seen again.'

Dora sighed. 'So did I, Cassie. But there's something going on, something in the air that I can't quite fathom. It has been building up for the last few weeks and now it's coming to a head.'

'On my birthday?'

'Yes.'

'Well then, it's a good job everyone will be here when it happens. You can do a few spells, my father can do whatever he does, Noel can summon up a bolt of lightning, and I'll zap them all with my lethal gemstones. Together, we'll be awesome.'

Cass had been joking, but when she saw her mother wasn't smiling she felt a chill right down to her bones.

'I hope awesome will be enough,' Dora said.

★ ★ ★

Cass woke up early on her birthday morning. A shaft of autumn sunshine fell across her bed. She sat up and took a deep breath of the spicy air coming in through the open window. Dora had planted herbs in the bed below, and the scent of mint and thyme seemed to be present all the year round. Today should be a happy day, she told herself, even though she was a year older and now fast approaching thirty.

Dora came in carrying a tray holding a teapot and two cups. 'Happy birthday, Cassie dear. I thought I might have a cup of tea with you this morning, then I'll make you breakfast. Whatever you want, as it's your special day. There's a little present on the tray,' she added.

Cass picked up a small black box. The ribbon tied round it sparkled with tiny lights. Cass undid the box while her mother poured the tea.

'I know they're only small,' Dora said, as Cass admired the earrings she had just taken from the box, 'but they are real sapphires, your birthstone, and they are more powerful than the ones in Rachel's necklace because these earrings are a gift given with love, and there is no power stronger than the power of love. They belonged to your grandmother, but they belong to you now, Cassie, and they will help protect you.' Cass sat quite still while her mother slipped the gold shaft through her ear, first one and then the other. 'Don't ever take them off, even when you wash your hair.'

Cass gave her mother a hug. 'I won't take them off,' she promised. 'Even if they don't go with my outfit, I'll still wear them.'

She was dying to ask about her grandmother, a woman she had never known, but Dora never talked about her family and was good at fielding any questions. She hadn't left the house for over six months, and Cass suspected her mother had a form of agoraphobia. She said Hector had put a spell on her, keeping her locked inside the house, and Cass decided that was one of the things she needed to talk to her father about. Not that she believed there was really a spell on her mother, but Dora believed in the spell and that was why it worked. The power of suggestion and all that.

She showered and dressed with extra care. If her mother was right, and this was the day she would meet her father face to face, she intended to look her very best. She rarely wore a dress — jeans and various tops being her usual mode of attire — but she knew she had dresses hidden away at the back of her wardrobe.

The dress she chose was a little red shift in a heavy silk that stopped just above her knees. Someone had once told her she had nice knees, so she thought she might as well show them off for once. It wasn't cold enough for tights, so she left her legs bare and slipped her feet into strappy black sandals with a small heel. Her hair she left loose. In the way of jewellery, she wore her new earrings and a small gold watch. She had wondered if her hair would clash with the colour of the dress, but a look in the mirror gave her a burst of confidence that she hoped would carry her through the rest of the day.

When she got downstairs she found her appetite had gone, so she asked her mother for a plain omelette. Dora sprinkled herbs on the omelette and poured fresh orange juice. She gave Cass a worried look. 'I told Noel to come for lunch. He said he'd put everything on hold today and come over as soon as he could. He should be here in an hour or so. You're not going to be on your own in this, Cassie.'

Cass's stomach baulked at the acidity of the juice so she drank half a glass of milk instead. Once her father turned up, she would be OK. It was the waiting that was getting her down. For all she knew, he might not come at all.

But half an hour later Hector Moon walked through the back door without bothering to knock.

Cass wasn't quite sure what she had been expecting. She knew her father wouldn't look the same as he had in the old photos. He thought he might have lost his hair, or become old and stooped like the wizards of her dreams, but this man still looked young and vibrant. He had changed, but not as much as she would've expected. He'd got rid of his beard and his hair was now lightly sprinkled with grey, but she would never forget his eyes. They were the most piercing blue she had ever seen.

He looked Dora up and down. 'You've put on weight since I saw you last.'

Dora gave him a peck on the cheek. 'I know. You told me I was too skinny.'

'It looks good on you.' He turned his attention to Cass, giving her the once-over with those amazing blue eyes. 'Happy birthday, Cassandra. You may not remember me, but I lived here in this house when you were a little girl.'

She shook her head. 'I don't remember you.'

'I know. I'm sorry you don't have any of those childhood memories, but I didn't take them away.'

Then who did? She wanted to believe him, but someone had been inside her head and removed all her early memories. Really important stuff. She needed to blame someone.

He pulled a small velvet bag from his pocket. 'I bought you a gift. You should have had it on your twenty-fifth birthday, but I didn't think you were ready.'

Another man making decisions for her. 'Thank you,' she said. 'But, like I said, I don't remember you at all; and Dora never talked about you, so perhaps she forgot about you as well. That's what happens when you go away and don't come back for years.' She knew she was being rude, but she couldn't help herself.

'I left because I believed I was bringing danger to you and your mother.'

'Then why come back?' He might be a commanding figure, Cass thought, but now she was facing him he didn't scare her anymore. He was flesh and bones, just like her. Not a monster hiding under her bed.

'Did you really think I was a monster?'

She refused to believe he could read her thoughts. 'Actually, I didn't think of you at all.'

'In reality, it doesn't make a tiny bit of difference what you think of me, Cassandra. I'm still your father and I still love you and your mother.' He smiled at her with no sign of irritation at her outburst. 'Open your present.'

The little bag was similar to the ones she used for her jewellery, but this bag held something very different. The ring was old, very old from the look of it: a heavy gold band engraved with strange symbols. In the centre sat a star sapphire. The stone was quite small, but the star seemed to be dead centre. She counted at least six rays of light emanating from the star, and that was without her loupe. She held the ring up to the light and frowned. Silk inclusions caused the star, usually, but this was different. When the sun's rays caught the stone at just the right angle, the star pulsed. Now Hector Moon had her attention.

'It's a natural star sapphire, isn't it?'

He nodded, watching her with a smile on his face. 'Your birthstone, Cassandra. But this stone is as old as time. It was in the ground when the first dinosaurs walked the earth. It was meant for you from the very beginning — and it will keep you safe.'

'My mother gave me sapphire earrings. They'll keep me safe.'

Her father took her right hand and slipped the ring on her finger. She felt it snuggle down as if it did, indeed, belong there. She wondered if it would be possible to take it off again.

'You need both of us to keep you safe right now, daughter, so I shall stay as long as I need.' He walked over to one of Dora's cupboards and took out a bottle. 'I know it's early, but I think we all need a drink.' He glanced down as Tobias jumped from the chair and came to stand beside him. 'How's the cat working out?'

'He's done everything he's supposed to,' Dora said. 'We had a black cat lurking outside the gate. One of Cassie's clients invited her in thinking she belonged to us, so she was able to slip past my defences. Tobias had a fight with her and saw her off, but I think she's back in the neighbourhood. I can sense when she's near. She's evil.'

Cass saw the drink in Hector's glass move slightly as his hand twitched. The man was quite impressive — he looked as if he could handle anything — but if *he* was nervous, then perhaps they should all be a bit worried.

13

Hector lifted the glass to his lips and took a sip of wine, his hand now quite steady. 'A female?' he asked. 'Was Raven here?'

'Not then,' Cass told him, 'but he was with me when we first saw the cat. He was scared of her, and Noel isn't scared of much. I wouldn't let her in, so she savaged me and ran off.' Cass pulled up her sleeve. 'I've still got the scars to prove it.'

'She's waiting for a more opportune moment. She won't give up.'

'You know her?' Dora asked.

'I know *of* her,' Hector said. 'There are very few of her kind around, and she'll be clever, but take away her talisman and she can do nothing.'

'What sort of talisman?' Cass asked. She couldn't imagine how a cat could carry anything with it. It could hardly have a lucky charm tucked away in a pocket somewhere. She suddenly remembered something. 'The cat was wearing a collar when I picked her up. Black leather, almost hidden in her fur, but I definitely felt a collar round her neck.'

'That's why she didn't want you to pick her up,' Dora said. 'She knew you'd feel it. But you can't just take the collar off. It will need some sort of magic to remove it.'

'Like a pair of scissors,' Cass said dryly. 'My nail scissors may not be magical, but they're damned sharp.' She looked at her father. 'What's so special about this cat?'

'She's probably a shape shifter,' he said casually as he refilled Cass's glass. 'They've been used in warfare for some time. A loyal soldier with an IQ of well over 150, who can change into a small black cat on demand, would be an asset to any faction.'

Cass took a deep breath, wondering how much longer she could suspend her disbelief. When the back door opened again and Noel walked in, she almost hugged him. Almost, but not quite.

He had one hand behind his back. 'I brought you a little present. I couldn't afford sapphires, but I think I got the colour right.' With a quick flourish he produced a posy of velvety blue pansies and handed them to her. 'Happy birthday, Cass.'

This time she did hug him, and even risked planting a quick kiss on his cheek.

'Thank you, Noel,' she said. 'I believe you've already met my father.'

Noel held out his hand. 'Agent Moore. Or is it Moon? Nice to meet you again.'

Hector smiled as he took the proffered hand. 'Did you guess, or were you told?'

'I told him it was you,' Dora said. 'I recognised you from Noel's description.'

Cass thought that was a bit odd considering her mother hadn't seen

Hector for over twenty years. If he hadn't changed his appearance in twenty years, he was probably immortal as well as everything else. Her sense of disbelief had more or less gone out of the window. Another glass of whatever was in the bottle and she'd believe anything.

She twisted the ring on her finger. She knew stones, and this was the best star sapphire she had ever seen, including the ones in various museum collections. For a moment she felt overwhelmed. Her father had found what was probably the most perfect stone in the whole world, and given it to her. The ring moved easily on her finger — until she tried to pull it off. Oh well, she thought philosophically, at least she wouldn't lose it.

'I may not be able to stay very long,' Hector said. 'Finchley won't tell me anything because he doesn't know anything, and he's really not that important. The people I'm working for at the moment are after the man at the top. This is no little local smuggling racket. It's a global organisation.'

'It certainly looks that way,' Noel agreed. 'But my involvement stops with the recovery of the stones and the arrest of the local man.'

'And I offered my services on this case because I needed to make sure my wife and daughter were safe.'

'The smugglers won't bother us again,' Dora said. 'But how about the hellcat? She went away, frightened off by Tobias, but now she's somewhere near again.'

'Then I will stay the night. The three of us together should be more than a match for the cat.' He smiled. 'I certainly don't need to leave until tomorrow. Besides, I would like to meet her.'

Cass shook her head. 'No, you wouldn't.'

'We should eat.' Dora took placemats from a drawer. 'An army can't march on an empty stomach.' Actually, she had no idea what an army had to do with anything. The four of them were hardly an army. Even if any of them *did* have special powers, so did the hellcat.

Cass helped her mother set the table, but her mind was only half on the task. Since her father had put the ring on her finger she felt different, and she was trying to work out why. She looked down at the ring and marvelled again at the number of rays emanating from the centre of the star. She was dying to get to her studio and use her loupe. The stone looked slightly misty, as it should, but instead of the star bouncing from the surface, it seemed to come from deep inside. She gave the ring a surreptitious pull, but it still wouldn't come off.

Halfway through the meal, Tobias climbed down from his chair and walked into the scullery. Dora watched him with a frown on her face. 'Something is bothering him. Something outside, I think.'

'Nothing can get in, Pandora,' Hector said soothingly. 'I've doubled the security.'

Once lunch was over and the table had been cleared, Hector opened his laptop computer, but the signal was too weak to pick up much. 'That's always a problem,' he said. 'Put up too much of a barrier and you can't get Wi-Fi. Pandora, do you have any books on black cats and their powers? If we can't get Google, we'll have to do our research the old-fashioned way.'

'I think I have several,' Dora said. 'I'll go and get them, but let me know when the internet connection comes back on. I need to order some envelopes for my recipes.'

As soon as she could, Cass made the excuse that she needed to check on some work in progress in her studio and told them she wouldn't be long. The men were too engrossed in their research to care where she went, and her mother was making more tea. She closed the door to the studio behind her and took out her loupe.

She was fascinated by the ring, and this time when she pulled at it, the heavy gold band slid off easily. She studied the symbols on either side of the stone. Pictures or letters, or just random marks engraved into the metal? It was difficult to tell. Some kind of cuneiform, maybe. She needed an expert on ancient writing to be sure. She sat back in her chair and stared at the strange little stone — a star so perfect, she had never seen one like it before. The other alternative was to ask her father, but she didn't want to do that. If this was some kind of test, she didn't intend to fail. He said the ring was ancient and the stone even older. Occasionally precious stones appear on the earth's surface, thrown up by tumultuous activity below the crust, but most are mined. All she had to do was find out the most likely source. At least that would be somewhere to start her investigation.

A knock on the outside door made her jump. She wasn't expecting anyone, and today was not a good day to call. Thinking it might be Rachel, she grabbed the ring and slipped it back on her finger before opening the door.

The woman standing in front of her couldn't have been much over five feet tall, but she was strikingly beautiful. Everything about her was petite. Her hair was shoulder-length and glossy black, her lips bright red, her eyes pure emerald green framed with long black lashes. She was carrying something in a plastic postbag.

'I met your postman at the gate, so I brought your parcel up here for you.' She handed Cass a package addressed to Pandora Moon. 'I was hoping to speak with Hector. I'm a friend of his, and I understand he's here at the moment.' She looked Cass up and down as if she were studying a rather insignificant specimen in a petri dish. 'I'm sure he'll want to see me. I've known him a long time.'

Cass had been feeling quite good about herself, but a staggeringly pretty little brunette had just taken away all of her confidence. Right now she felt fat and ugly. She was sure she had gained a couple of stone in the last few seconds. The ring felt tight on her finger and her dress had ridden up her thighs. She pulled at her hemline anxiously, wondering what was wrong with her.

'May I come in?' the woman said.

Cass stood back from the door feeling stupid. She wasn't usually this ill-mannered. 'Yes, of course,' she said. 'Please come in.' She realised her mistake instantly, but it was too late to do anything about it. The woman stepped over the threshold with a little purr of satisfaction.

'I didn't think it would be this easy,' she said. 'I thought you were quite a clever girl, Cassandra, but that little spell always works wonders. Demoralising, isn't it?' She looked round the studio and smiled. 'All those lovely gems that might possibly have come to your aid are safely locked away, I see. What a pity. It looks as if you are all on your own.' She smoothed her mane of black hair with a hand tipped with long red talons and purred again. A particularly feline sound. 'Shall we go and find dear Hector and your darling mother? I'm so looking forward to meeting them.'

Cass didn't know whether she had any options left. Even if she did, she couldn't think of anything that would work. The safest place, surely, was in a room full of people with magical powers. What was the point of having a witch for a mother and a warlock for a father if they couldn't send this creature packing? Add Tobias to the mix and they might all stand a chance.

'Of course,' she said politely. 'Follow me.'

When Cass opened the door into the kitchen they were standing in a row, facing her — Dora in the middle, the two men either side.

The woman clapped her hands. 'Oh, how lovely. A reception committee. Now I feel really welcome. I've been waiting a long time to meet you all. I was delighted when Cassandra so graciously invited me into your home.'

Cass felt mortified. There was nothing she could do or say that would take away her feeling of guilt. 'I'm so sorry,' she said in a small voice.

Dora ignored the visitor and put an arm round her daughter. 'It wasn't your fault, Cassie. Like Hector said, she's clever.'

The woman purred again. 'Not only do I get to visit your lovely home, but now I'm getting compliments as well.'

'That wasn't a compliment, Margot,' Hector said quietly. 'You look a lot older than when I saw you last. Every time you shape shift, you lose another of your nine lives. You must be getting near the end of your time.' He turned to Cass. 'She half-French,' he said. 'She comes from a distant line of French shape shifters called Matagots. All they used to want back then was a warm bed and a chicken now and again.' He sighed. 'How times have changed.'

Noel had moved up beside Cass and now he took her hand in his. She felt the first tingle of electricity in the tips of her fingers and looked at him curiously. He shook his head slightly, and then nodded towards the woman, who was still talking to Hector. 'We can do this together,' he whispered.

Tobias was still sitting on his chair. His ears were pricked and the ruff of fur round his neck was standing on end, but he didn't move. Margot saw where Cass was looking. 'He can't hurt me while I look like this.' She put up her hand and touched something at her neck. Cass saw that the woman was wearing an ornate pendant on a strip of leather. The pendant wasn't a gemstone but metal of some sort, twisted into a series of interlocking rings. Her talisman.

Cass had a feeling her manicure scissors weren't going to work.

Noel was holding her right hand and she could feel heat from the ring Hector had given her. Margot had said she didn't have the protection of her gemstones — but she did: the star sapphire on her finger and the tiny gems in her ears. Even as the thought entered her head she felt the electricity, almost painful in its intensity, beginning to pulse through her whole body. Noel grinned at her, and then with a triumphant shout they raised their joined hands in the air.

Cass screamed as the blast forced their hands apart. The place where the woman had been standing was empty, and for a moment Cass expected to see a pile of ashes on the floor. Surely nothing could withstand a bolt of lightning that powerful. Her breath caught in her throat. She knew the woman was dangerous, but she didn't want to be responsible for her death.

Tobias was on his feet, facing a corner of the room, his teeth bared and his tail twitching. It took Cass a moment, but then she spotted the black cat backed into the corner, smoke still rising from a red mark on her flank. She spat at Tobias and leapt straight up onto the curtain rail above the window. It sagged a little under her weight, but Cass knew it was bolted securely to the wall. Tobias climbed back on to his chair and stood watching her.

Dora coughed, and Cass turned to look at her mother.

Hector moved quickly, catching the little witch as she fell. 'Get that animal before it kills her,' he shouted at Noel, but Tobias had already sprung up from his chair and landed beside the black cat. The wooden rail couldn't take the double weight. It snapped in the middle, sending both animals crashing to the ground. Now they were locked together; an obscene ball of hissing, spitting fur that shot around the room like some demented creature from a horror movie. Now and again they would separate, but it was impossible to tell who was winning the fight.

Noel started towards them, but Cass called out to him. 'Wait, Noel. She'll savage you. We have to get her collar.'

The hellcat buried her teeth in Tobias's soft underbelly and he screamed, a long drawn-out howl that only a cat can make. Cass wasn't going to wait any longer. The creature causing all the anguish wasn't much more than a foot long, a pussy cat, and Cass was angry now. Very angry. No one was allowed to hurt her mother — or their cat.

She waited until the two animals were within range, and then bent down and grabbed the black cat by the scruff of its neck. She ignored the bloody claws that reached for her face and felt through the thick fur for the collar. A long, hooked talon pierced her skin just below her eye and she nearly let go, but Tobias was doing his best to help. He grabbed the hellcat's ear with his teeth and she squealed with pain.

Cass had to cut the collar off the hellcat's neck, but scissors weren't going to do the job, even if she had a pair handy. She could feel her ring pulsing on her finger like a heartbeat. It wasn't only the hellcat that had a talisman. Hoping she was doing the right thing, she pressed the star sapphire against the cat's collar and closed her eyes.

There was no blast of lightning this time — only a small *ping* as the collar broke in two. The hellcat screamed with rage, but it was too late. Cass unhooked the claw from her face and sat back on her heels. She looked at the creature in front of her, reduced now to nothing but a small black cat shivering with fear, and felt a pang of guilt. But as Noel helped her to her feet she glimpsed her mother, laid out pale and motionless on the floor, and any feelings of remorse disappeared.

She ran over to Dora, leaving Tobias guarding the black cat, and squatted down on the floor beside Hector. 'Is she going to be all right?'

He had his hand on Dora's forehead. 'Yes, I think so. Her colour is coming back and she's breathing again.'

'She stopped breathing?' Cass felt her own breath almost stop. Noel lifted her to her feet and for a moment she clung to him. 'We did it, didn't we? We defeated her.'

He tipped up her chin and kissed her. 'Together we are invincible. How does that sound?'

'Like something out of a Marvel comic. A bit stupid, really. But I know what you mean, and it feels good.'

14

Hector lifted Dora in his arms and laid her down on the sofa. 'Pandora should go to bed. She needs to rest.'

Dora sat up.' 'I'm not going to bed. I missed most of the drama, didn't I? What happened to the hellcat?'

Hector pushed Dora back down on the sofa with a firm hand. 'Do lie down, Pandora. She almost killed you. She lost her power when Cass broke her collar, and now she's just a poor little moggy.' He smiled. 'I know someone at a cat rescue shelter who'll take her in, and if she's a good little pussycat she might get a warm bed and some chicken. Just what she always wanted.'

Ignoring Hector, Dora swung her legs round and sat up. 'There's a cat basket in the scullery. Put her in that, Cassie, and Tobias won't have to stand guard over her. His wound needs dressing, and we all need a cup of tea.'

Before she could stand up, Hector put his hand on her shoulder. 'Do what you're told for once, Pandora, and sit down. I'll make the tea.'

'And I'll put the cat in the basket,' Noel said. 'The women have done enough. They both need to sit down.'

Cass dropped onto the sofa beside her mother. 'Who are we to argue?' She took Dora's hand in hers. 'Don't ever do that again, Mum. You scared me.'

'I think I scared myself.' Dora still sounded a little shaky. 'She's really powerful.'

Cass shook her head. 'No, she isn't. Her talisman was powerful, but the ring Hector gave me is even better. Noel helped me make her change her shape, and then Tobias took her on. Between us we backed her into a corner.' She looked down at the ring on her finger. 'The star sapphire is my talisman, isn't it? That's why my father wanted me to have it. So I could save you.'

Dora sighed and leaned back against

275

the cushions. 'At one time I could have saved myself, but magic is a little bit like modern technology — it keeps upgrading itself. I'm slipping behind; so is your father. You and Noel are the new generation. You have to take over from us.'

Cass smiled. 'And save the world?'

'Something like that.'

Noel came back into the room with the cat in a basket. 'What do we do with the broken collar?' he asked Hector. 'Does it still have any power?'

Hector put a tray with a teapot and cups on the table and went to the refrigerator for milk. 'I honestly don't know, but I have an insulated box in my car specially made for things like that.'

'Like the one they used in *Ghostbusters*?' Cass asked. She hadn't the energy to be sceptical any longer. Everything had become so surreal that she was beginning to feel like Alice. If they all sat round the kitchen table it would be like the Mad Hatter's tea party. She left her mother on the sofa and helped her father pour the tea.

Hector persuaded Dora to lie down in her bedroom, but Cass felt too wired to rest. Hector thanked her for the tea and said he would have to leave. Noel asked if he wanted to take Finchley with him, but he shook his head.

'I don't think Finchley knows anything that will help the organisation I work for. The smuggling group keeps the different operatives segregated from one another, so no one person knows more than they absolutely have to. Dempsey was just a pawn, too far down the chain for them to bother about. They won't like losing Finchley, just in case he knows more than they think he does, but they won't come after him. It would be too much trouble.'

He turned and looked at Cass. 'I'm after someone who has nothing to do with the smuggling ring. I don't know him, but I know he doesn't like me. That doesn't bother me. What does bother me is that he's involved my wife and daughter in something that has nothing to do with them. And in doing that, he's made it personal.'

Cass frowned. She looked at the basket, and a small black cat that didn't look capable of swatting a fly. 'You think the hellcat was working for someone else?'

'I know she was. Margot is a spy — that's her job — and the only reason she would be here in this house is because she was spying on you. Your powers are just beginning to blossom, Cassandra. You are an unknown force. I think someone, or some*thing*, wants to know exactly who you are and what you can do. But if you keep a low profile for a while things will quieten down.'

'Do you think this someone will come looking for the hellcat?' Noel asked.

Hector shrugged. 'I doubt it. If she's been foolish enough to get herself caught, then she's not worth the trouble.' He smiled at Cass. 'You'll be safe for a while, daughter. You and your mother.'

'Thank you,' Cass said. She wondered if she should give him a hug. She did have a lot to thank him for. But he saved her any embarrassment by folding her in his arms. 'I missed you, Cassandra. We used to have fun together.'

'Then let me remember those times. And let my mother go free. She needs to get out of this house. She's not an old lady yet.'

'I didn't do anything to keep your mother in the house. She needed somewhere safe after she was attacked, a sanctuary, and agoraphobia has kept her safe. She can go outside whenever she wishes. Tell her I'm sorry for all the heartache I caused her — will probably still cause her — but she knew what she was getting into when she married me. She's asleep right now, and I'm not going to wake her, but tell her I still love her.' He gave Cass a final kiss on the cheek and held out his hand to Noel. 'Look after my daughter for me while I'm gone.' He picked up the cat basket and turned towards the door.

And then he disappeared.

Cass was sure he had opened the

door and left in a perfectly normal manner, but her eyes were blurred with tears and she didn't actually see him go. She felt a sense of anti-climax. Her father had gone and so had the hellcat. Tobias was back on his favourite chair, nonchalantly washing his face, and her mother was in bed. The house seemed abnormally quiet. She saw Noel watching her with a curious expression on his face.

'It's over, Cass. You can relax now.'

'Can I?' She didn't feel relaxed. She felt alone.

'Shall I get us a drink?'

So she could drown her sorrows? Why not? 'Yes please, and thank you for coming over.' She gave him a weak little smile. 'I couldn't have done it without you.'

'No, you couldn't, could you? You need me, Cass, even if you won't admit it.'

He rummaged in her mother's cupboard and found a bottle of wine. Cass watched him fill two glasses and hoped it really was wine and not one of her mother's strange concoctions. As she took the glass from him their fingers touched. There was no fizz of electricity this time and she felt her body start to relax, but she only had time to take one sip of her wine before he took the glass away from her again. She looked at him in confusion. 'What are you doing, Noel? I want my drink back.'

'No, you don't. Not yet.' He put the glass down on the table and took her hand. 'I have a little experiment I want to try out. Close your eyes and count to ten.'

She backed away warily. What was he up to now? 'Why? What are you going to do?'

'Trust me, Cassandra. Just this once, pretend I'm your best friend and you trust me completely. Can you do that?'

Could she do that? She wasn't really sure. If she were totally honest, she did trust Noel, but she wasn't entirely sure she could trust herself.

He was standing looking at her expectantly — a tall, darkly handsome man who had once saved her life. He had definitely proved himself a friend, but she didn't want him as a friend. She wanted a whole lot more than that. More than he was prepared to give. She hadn't really got a lot to lose, so she took a deep breath and closed her eyes.

'Make your mind blank,' he said quietly, and for a moment she wondered if he were going to try and hypnotise her.

He was very close now, and she could feel the warmth of his body next to hers, his breath on her cheek. Even the faint scent of lemon aftershave. His lips brushed hers and she felt a tingle right down to her toes, but this time it was different. This time it was like a harp string being plucked somewhere deep inside her body — a tiny thrill of pleasure that built in intensity as his mouth covered hers. He pulled her against him and the notes of the harp sang in her ears, a sound that was almost painful.

Her body felt soft and fluid. Any moment now she was going to collapse in a bone-less heap on the floor.

She opened her eyes and pulled away from him, breaking the connection.

He smiled at her. 'See? It worked.'

'What worked?' Her legs were still weak and she wanted to lie down, but that might be a mistake right now.

'We didn't start an electrical storm, did we? Or blow one another up with a lightning bolt. Your father told me what to do if I wanted to get close to you. He knows you better than you think.'

'You told my father you wanted to get close to me?' she asked incredulously. 'What else did you tell him? He's my father, and I hardly know the man, but you're telling him your most intimate secrets.'

Noel laughed. 'Good heavens, no. My most intimate secrets are enough to shock anyone, even a warlock.' He led her to the sofa and pulled her down beside him. 'We're a team, Cass. We need one another, you know that as well as I do, and all that sexual tension was starting to drive us apart.'

'Is that what it was? Sexual tension? I thought you wanted to be my friend.'

'That was a friendly kiss, wasn't it?'

'Oh, yes,' she said. 'Very friendly.' She turned to face him and looked into those gorgeous quicksilver eyes. 'If you want us to be friends, don't try that experiment again.'

He sighed. 'I'm sorry. I shouldn't have pushed you, but the frustration is killing me. I've wanted to kiss you since the moment I first saw you, but I was afraid of hurting you; giving you an electric shock or something. You have a habit of collapsing if I get a bit too close, and I didn't know what would happen if I kissed you. At this precise moment spontaneous combustion seems a distinct possibility. If we start off being friends, then maybe everything else will sort itself out naturally. You must know how I feel about you.'

She opened her eyes wide with surprise. 'No, I don't. That's just the point. I thought you weren't interested.'

'I'm a very good actor. I didn't want to frighten you away.'

'I'm a grown woman, Noel, not a scared little girl, and I'm not afraid of you. Not anymore. What we have is amazing. You've heard all those stories about the earth moving? Well, maybe they're not stories. Just think what we might be able to do together.'

He began to move closer to her but she put a hand on his chest. 'Not now, Noel. Like you said, anything could happen.'

'I'm willing to take my chances.'

There was a predatory look in his eye and she was just beginning to wonder if she ought to make a run for it, when the door opened and Dora walked in.

Cass felt her face go warm. That was the trouble when you lived with your mother. Very little chance of privacy. She was glad her mother had come in sooner rather than later, though, or it could have been even more embarrassing.

Dora looked round the room with sleepy eyes. 'Has he gone?'

'Hector didn't want to wake you.' Cass helped her mother into a chair. 'He said to tell you he still loves you.'

Dora smiled. 'I know that. He didn't need to tell me. He loves you, too, Cassie. He just has . . . '

'A strange way of showing it.' Cass nodded. 'I know. He told Noel to look after me while he's away.'

'And Noel will,' Dora said. 'I can see it in his eyes. Something has changed. Whatever the problem was between you two, it has gone, and you are both much stronger.' She frowned. 'What happened to the cat? Did Hector take her?'

'He's dropping her off at a rescue shelter where she'll get a warm bed and chicken,' Noel told her. 'Shall I get you a drink, Dora?'

Dora sighed with pleasure. 'Thank you, Noel. I love you, Cassie, but it is nice to have a man around sometimes, isn't it?'

Cass felt her face starting to get hot

again. 'Noel opened one of your bottles of wine. We thought we should celebrate our victory.'

'Put the wine away.' Dora got to her feet and took a bottle of champagne from the refrigerator. 'This is what we need for a victory celebration. Can one of you open it for me?'

'As stand-in man about the house,' Noel said, 'I'm offering my services as chief champagne bottle opener.'

The house phone started to ring and Dora looked at it in surprise. She picked it up and handed the receiver to Cass. 'It's Rachel.'

Cass couldn't imagine what the woman was calling about. Dempsey was out of hospital and probably living with her by now. No charges had been brought against the man, even though they all knew he was guilty of smuggling precious stones out of America. Cass pushed the connect button and put the phone to her ear.

'Hi, Cass. Your mobile isn't picking up.'

Rachel sounded nervous, which made Cass nervous. What had happened now? Nothing else could go wrong, surely. 'My mobile phone got broken, but it's lovely to hear from you. Is everything OK?'

'Yes, it is. More than OK. I have some wonderful news. Chris has asked me to marry him.'

'Wow, that *is* good news.' Cass hoped it was, but she had her doubts. Noel was trying to listen in over her shoulder and she pushed him away.

'We've decided to go and live in Spain.' Rachel said. 'We both feel we need a fresh start, and they love British nurses in places like Benidorm. They have lots of British holidaymakers and expats, so I can get a job there easily. Chris is going to open a beach bar.'

'When is the wedding?' Cass asked. Noel was still hovering, so she pulled a face at him and moved the phone to her other ear.

'We don't know yet. But Chris gave me the most beautiful engagement ring.

It belonged to his mother.'

'I wish you both all the luck in the world,' she told Rachel. The woman was probably going to need it. Cass was worried Dempsey might have a few things in his past that were going to surface at some time and get him into trouble all over again. Perhaps it would be a good thing if the pair did leave the country for a while.

'I really phoned to ask if you and your mother would like to come to our anniversary party. Liz will be there, and some of the other hospital staff that you already know. You're welcome to bring your boyfriend. I know he's a policeman, but he let Chris off with a caution, and we're really grateful to him for that.'

'There was no evidence against Chris,' Cass said, crossing her fingers. 'I'll speak to my mother, but I'm sure Noel would love to come. You can ask him yourself, if you like. He's right here beside me.' She held the phone out to Noel. 'Rachel wants to ask you to her engagement party.'

The expression on his face made her want to giggle, not something she did very often. She watched his expression change again as he listened to Rachel. 'I think that's a lovely idea. It will do Pandora good to get out of the house. I'll run us all there in my car.' He said goodbye and put the phone down. 'That was a surprise.'

Dora looked up from her seat on the sofa. 'You know I can't go out, Noel.'

'We've all been invited to Rachel's engagement party. I think you can go outside the garden now, Dora. You should give it a try. You've been locked in long enough.'

Cass saw the emotions flit across her mother's face before Dora got to her feet. 'I haven't been outside for over six months, but I'd like to see Rachel and make sure that smuggler will make her happy.'

Noel was about to say something, but Cass gave him a warning look. 'Before my father left, he told me he'd removed his spell. He only did it to keep you safe. He didn't want you to feel like a prisoner, so he took the spell away. You can go out now whenever you want.'

Dora still looked apprehensive. 'I'll give it a try, Cassie, but not tonight. When is the party, Noel?'

At the weekend, so you've still got a few days to make up your mind. A party would do you good, Dora.'

Pandora Moon smiled at him. 'Perhaps it would.'

15

The day was bright and sunny, another lovely autumn day. A great day for a party, Cass thought. Even better if she could get her mother to go as well.

Hector had been right — her mother's reluctance to leave the house had nothing to do with spells and everything to do with the trauma she had suffered at the hands of her attackers. She had been walking back to the house on a balmy spring evening when a gang of youths started pelting her with stones. From what Cass could gather when she visited her mother in hospital, they were shouting at her, calling her a witch and saying she deserved a stoning. Probably because they couldn't burn her at the stake or drown her in a pond, Cass thought bitterly. Dora had been hit on the head with the first rock and knocked unconscious, unable to protect herself, even with magic.

Now she had promised Cass she would try and walk to the end of the drive, and Cass felt as nervous as her mother.

'Do stop fussing, Cassie.' Dora had replaced her usual flat mules with ankle boots, and thrown a thick shawl over her brightly coloured caftan. 'Put a coat on, child, and let's get on with it.'

Usually Cass used the back gate out of the little patio, but that led to a rough patch of grass and bushes and Dora had promised to walk to the end of the drive, so that was what they would do. She opened the front door, grateful for the sunshine. The driveway looked bright and unthreatening to her, but she wasn't sure how her mother would see it. Normally, if Dora went any further than the grounds of the house she felt faint and unable to breathe.

Dora pulled her shawl more tightly round her and took a deep breath. As

Cass reached out to take her mother's arm, the little witch stepped over the threshold and walked down the two small steps onto the driveway. She turned to smile up at her daughter. 'You didn't believe me when I said Hector put a spell on me, did you? Well, this proves I was right, doesn't it?'

Cass had no intention of arguing with her mother. She was so pleased to see Dora walking amongst the crisp fallen leaves, she would have agreed to anything. Hector had said he had nothing to do with Dora being confined to the house, but she knew her father was capable of lying, and sometimes it was difficult to know what to believe.

'It feels wonderful to be outside the garden,' Dora said happily. 'Now I can dress up and go to Rachel's party.'

'You must promise not to go anywhere on your own to start with,' Cass said worriedly, wondering why she had been so keen to get Dora to go out. Up until now she had always known exactly where her mother was. 'You mustn't rush it. You have to take things one step at a time.'

'Oh, do stop fussing, Cassie. Walk with me to the end of the drive and then we'll go back inside and open a bottle of champagne to celebrate.'

Cass thought it was a bit early for champagne, but that wasn't worth an argument, either. This really was a day to celebrate.

The phone was ringing as they walked into the kitchen. Cass picked up the receiver, smiling at her mother's flushed and happy face. She had known it would be Noel even before he spoke.

'How did the rehearsal go?' he asked.

Cass laughed. 'All the way to the end of the drive and back, according to plan. Now we're celebrating with champagne.'

'Good for you. I wish I could come over, but I have to work this morning. I'll pick you both up about eight this evening. I don't suppose your mother will want to stay too long if it's her first time out.'

'I'm not so sure about that. She looks raring to go at the moment. I forgot to ask where we're going. Is it formal or informal?' Having met Rachel and Chris, Cass wasn't sure what sort of venue the pair might choose.

'Informal, I would imagine. The party is at the Rising Sun. Eight to whenever. Closing time, I would imagine.'

The Rising Sun was an obvious choice. Rachel was a nurse and most of the staff from the hospital frequented the pub at one time or another. She was glad it wasn't some formal, over-the-top, posh do where she would have to dress up.

Dora spent most of the afternoon experimenting with different outfits, all of which involved a kaftan of some sort. Cass thought her mother looked like a foreign princess. The kaftan was mostly gold and red with just a touch of brilliant royal blue. She had jewelled sandals on her small feet and a long cashmere shawl to throw around her shoulders.

She looked at Cass and shook her

head. 'You're not going dressed like that.'

It sounded more like an order than a question, which annoyed Cass a little. Her mother didn't have any right to criticise her clothes. She wasn't a child anymore. Cass thought she looked quite reasonable. The jeans were from some designer shop when they'd had a half-price sale, and her top was a fairly new sweater in pale grey.

'It's a pub, Mother. Everyone wears jeans to a pub, even if it's a party.'

'That's just fine. I can understand that. So why do you look as if you're going to a funeral?'

Cass sighed. She felt like a naughty child who wouldn't be allowed out of the house until she changed her clothes. Which she knew from experience was probably true.

'How about the red silk top, Cassie? You'll look lovely in that, even if you insist on wearing it with jeans.'

When Cass came back downstairs, Noel was waiting in the kitchen. 'Aren't

I the lucky man,' he said gallantly.

Cass was a bit worried about getting her mother in a car again after so long, but Dora seemed quite excited at the idea of an evening out.

The Rising Sun was crowded, with music going full blast, and Rachel the centre of attention. She looked radiantly happy with Chris at her side, and Cass had to admit they looked good together. She could imagine them living it up in Spain or on one of the Greek islands. Good luck to both of them, she thought as she followed Noel into the pub. She noticed he had tucked Dora's arm through his as though he was worried about losing her.

Rachel had been true to her word and had only invited a few close friends, mostly from the hospital; and Chris seemed to be getting on well with everyone. Liz was in the middle of a group of men and obviously enjoying herself. Her skirt stopped several inches above her knees, and the bright red of her clinging top matched her lipstick.

Cass was beginning to feel decidedly underdressed. Her mother had been right again.

Rachel was waving her hand around, showing off her new engagement ring. Cass smiled when she saw it. A pale blue sapphire surrounded by small diamonds.

'I doubt it belonged to Chris's mother,' she said to Noel, 'because it's a very modern setting. But I'm sure Rachel loves it, and it's a nice thought giving her a sapphire to replace the ones you took away.'

'Not stolen, I hope.'

'No, it's a pretty little stone, but not very valuable.'

Noel laughed. 'If you think about it, Dempsey actually won in the end. He got the girl and a sapphire. He probably bought it with the proceeds from his trip to Miami, but good luck to him. I had to let him go because I didn't have enough evidence to keep him locked up.'

'It's a shame Rachel had to give up

her sapphires. She really loved them.'

'I couldn't let her keep them, Cass. You know that.'

She smiled at him. 'I do know that, but they really looked amazing in the setting I made. I was so proud of my work.'

'So you should be.' He took her hand and held it up to the light. 'The ring your father gave you is amazing, too. Perhaps I should get you one for the other hand.'

He was watching Dora across the room as she sipped a cocktail and chatted to Rachel, so Cass couldn't see his face.

'For the other hand?'

'Yes.' Now he turned to look at her, his eyes a smoky grey in the dim light. 'I was told you get a substantial dowry when you get married. I don't want to miss out on anything.'

She tried to pull her hand away, but he held on tight and she could feel the electricity fizzing. 'Let go of my hand, Noel. We're going to cause a disturbance if we disappear in a flash of lightning.

Besides, I don't get the money until I'm thirty.'

He lifted her hand to his lips and kissed her palm. 'I can wait.'

She looked at him. 'We won this time, but is it all over?'

He put his arm round her. 'It's never going to be over, Cass. But we're getting there.'

We do hope that you have enjoyed reading this large print book.

Did you know that all of our titles are available for purchase?

We publish a wide range of high quality large print books including:
**Romances, Mysteries, Classics
General Fiction
Non Fiction and Westerns**

Special interest titles available in large print are:
**The Little Oxford Dictionary
Music Book, Song Book
Hymn Book, Service Book**

Also available from us courtesy of Oxford University Press:
**Young Readers' Dictionary
(large print edition)
Young Readers' Thesaurus
(large print edition)**

For further information or a free brochure, please contact us at:
**Ulverscroft Large Print Books Ltd.,
The Green, Bradgate Road, Anstey,
Leicester, LE7 7FU, England.
Tel:** (00 44) **0116 236 4325
Fax:** (00 44) **0116 234 0205**

STORM CHASER

Paula Williams

When Caitlin Mulryan graduates from university and returns to Stargate, the small Dorset village where she grew up, she is dismayed to find that the longstanding feud between her family and the Kingtons is as fierce as ever. Soon her twin brother is hunted down in his boat *Storm Chaser* by his bitter enemy, with tragedy in their wake — and Caitlin can only blame herself for her foolish actions. So falling in love with handsome Yorkshireman Nick Thorne is the last thing on her mind . . .

THE PARADISE ROOM

Sheila Spencer-Smith

The stone hut on the cliffs holds special memories for Nicole, who once spent so many happy hours within its walls — so when she has the chance to purchase it, she is ecstatic. Then the past catches up with her when Connor, the itinerant artist she fell in love with all those years ago, reappears in her life. But has his success changed him? And what of Daniel, the charismatic sculptor she has recently met? Nicole's heart finds itself torn between past and present . . .

FINN'S FOREST

Margaret Mounsden

When her son Gareth wins a competition for a stay in Finn's Forest, Eirlys Pendragon is at first thrilled, and charmed by its owner, Finn Hart. But it's anything but plain sailing as the manicured and tactless Miranda, wife of the camp's wealthy financier, takes an instant dislike to Eirlys, and her bullying son singles out Gareth. Eirlys believes the only way to deal with fear is to face up to it — but flying down a zip wire into Finn's arms seems an extreme solution to the problem . . .

EMBRACEABLE YOU

Suzanne Ross-Jones

Chrissy Grieves is good at her job at McGregor's Transport, and works hard — which leaves her little time for relationships. Besides, she's been unlucky in love, and her mother hasn't exactly been the best role model in that department. So when the boss's son, Mark, is brought home to keep an eye on the business while his parents are on holiday, the last thing Chrissy expects is to fall for him — and she's determined to keep her distance. Can Mark persuade her to take a chance on love?